Stolen Kisses

RENEE HARLESS

Stolen Kisses

RENEE HARLESS

Sara Campbell doesn't *do* relationships. As a divorce lawyer, she's witnessed one too many failed marriages and has zero plans to add herself as another statistic.

Cooper Divers has enough on his plate as a local detective and doesn't have time for a relationship. Fun is the name of the game for him.

From the first time they meet Sara and Cooper are like oil and water, pitching verbal jabs at each other for their own entertainment.

But when they're thrown together as the best man and maid of honor, the undeniable spark and heat between them ignites.

It doesn't take long for Cooper to realize that he's willing to toss away his rules on relationships. Can he convince Sara to do the same and take a chance on love?

Chapter One

Sara

H IS BEADY EYES STARE at me from across the table, and I can see that behind them he is silently undressing me as his lawyer tries to persuade me to negotiate better terms. He makes me sick, they all do. People see my long blonde hair and shapely curves tucked away beneath my suits, and they automatically think one of two things – either I'm a bimbo who breezed through law school because of her looks or that I can be their new sugar momma. Neither of those options is the case for me. I busted my ass through law school to graduate with honors and I had a job waiting for me the day I passed my boards.

"No, Mr. Delecheck. My client has zero interest in changing her request for child support. Mr. Stable gave up his rights for custody and visitation for his children, but that doesn't mean he isn't obligated to support them financially."

Since I helped my best friend Elle through her nasty divorce, it seems that I keep seeing the same cases over and over. And I am seriously considering stepping back as a senior partner at the firm. A job that I worked tirelessly to achieve, but the only difference seems to be a corner office with longer hours.

I can't even remember the last time I went out on a date. Hell, I can't remember the last time I picked up someone at a bar. That's my usual MO. After witnessing so many marriages fall apart, I have zero interest in heading down the matrimonial path.

Mr. Delecheck continues to drone on, sounding like the adults in the old *Charlie Brown* cartoons. If he keeps this up the headache forming at the base of my head is going to turn into a full-blown migraine.

"I'm going to tell you one final time, my client is not going to adjust her requests. If we can't settle this here, today, then we will see you in court where a judge will decide for you. And I am certain neither you nor your client is going to be happy with that outcome."

I watch gleefully as the lawyer's face blanches at my statement. In this jurisdiction, it is well known that the judge is a stickler when there are children involved in a divorce. She and I share the same sentiments. When Elle got divorced from her cheating scumbag of a husband, I made sure the first thing we did was settle an arrangement for her two amazing kids. She had a booming business and didn't need anything from her ex; all she wanted was the kids.

Ten minutes later, I stand with my client as we shake hands with her ex, his lawyer, and the mediator. Mr. Delecheck scoffs as he passes their signed papers over to the mediator to turn into the courts. I can tell that he hates the fact that my client and I wouldn't budge to his demands but instead had to cower toward ours.

I'm ruthless and I demand respect for myself and my clients so if they want something in the divorce and I find it reasonable, you can bet your ass I'm going to make sure that it happens. That's one thing about me that the other partners at the firm hate – I am not afraid to tell my clients when they're being unreasonable. It's why I have the most substantial client list at the firm as well. I'm always fair.

"Well, congratulations, Tasha, I think that went very well."

The woman throws her arms around my neck, a common occurrence after a final meeting, and thanks me numerous times.

"You're welcome. Now go home and take your kids out for ice cream. And I expect a Christmas card around the holidays."

"You got it!" she shouts as she hurries out of the conference room and out of the building.

Back in my office, I start sifting through the files on my desk. A few are potential clients I've had contact me directly, and a few are clients that my colleagues brushed aside and handed off to me because they'd rather spend their work hours on the golf course. A particular file at the bottom of the stack catches my eye and I groan as I flip through the paperwork.

Pressing the intercom button on my desk phone, I reach out to the secretary. "Janice, can you tell me why the Cullan case is sitting on my desk?"

"Um. . .Ms. Campbell, I believe Mr. Nemmer placed it there thinking you'd be a better fit for it."

"And where is Mr. Nemmer now?"

I can hear the hesitation in her voice at my question. We both know he isn't in the office; I'm the only one here this late on a Friday afternoon – every Friday afternoon.

"He left a little before lunch."

"Mmhmm. Thanks, Janice. Why don't you head home for the evening? I'll close up. Seems I'll be here later than I expected."

"Oh, that would be lovely. Thanks. Enjoy your weekend."

I release the intercom button on the phone and seriously consider taking the folder and placing it back on

Mr. Nemmer's desk. The slimy weasel has done this three times since I received my promotion. He hates to get his hands dirty in challenging cases, and the Cullan divorce is everything but neat and tidy.

Highlighter in hand, I start reading through the cases, notating certain parts that we need to address during the client meetings. Before I know it, the sky has changed from a breathtaking orange hue to a darkness only illuminated by the glow of the side street lamp located outside my window. Glancing down at the corner of my computer screen I groan when I see the number change to 8:51 p.m.

I consider leaving the files on my desk to tackle on Monday, but I know myself too well. I'd be back tomorrow morning to grab them and work. When you're single and without a Netflix account you pretty much rely on work to keep you busy – or at least I do.

Grabbing a flimsy cardboard file box from the bottom row of the shelving unit behind my desk, I place the various files into the divided slots and then replace the top. Reaching into my desk drawer, I grab my purse and sling it over my shoulder then cradle the box against my chest as I exit my office.

The ride from my office to my apartment is short. I speed through a few stoplights and pull into my condo parking lot and heft the heavy box into my arms. Trudging up the steps I'm relieved when I don't see Phil, my obnoxious neighbor. Though he means well, he tends to overstep the barriers of personal space.

Once inside I place the box on my coffee table and stroll into my kitchen, ignoring the desire to begin working on the files. I force myself to choke down a frozen dinner, hating the fact that I missed going to the store to stock up on groceries. Cooking is one of my favorite things to do when I have free nights, which seems to be less and less these days.

Grabbing my phone from my purse, I shoot a text to Elle to see what she's up to tonight. But I already know the answer. She and her neighbor Jackson are now an official couple, and that means she doesn't have much time left for me, especially since her two kids are growing up by the day.

"Ugh, snap out of it, Sara," I murmur to myself.

In my heart I know that I have my reasons for staying out of relationships, but it doesn't make it any easier to see everyone around me happy. Stealing a glance over at the brown box sticking out like a sore thumb amongst my light colored décor, I remember the relationships that I've watched crumble before my eyes.

Thanking the heavens that I live alone, I remove my shoes and suit jacket and skirt, leaving me in a silk camisole and panties. Next, I untwist the knot on the back of my head and let my wavy blonde hair spill over my shoulders. Falling back on the couch, I tuck my feet beneath me and settle in for some reality television. The endless drivel is enough for my brain to turn off and stop thinking about work and why I feel like my life has taken a wrong turn somewhere.

A loud crash sounds from outside my apartment and I realize that I've fallen asleep on the couch with the remote still in my hand. Reaching my arms toward the ceiling, I stretch before noticing the clock on the wall reads 2 a.m. Great. With a hearty spoonful of hope, I trudge back to my bedroom and pull back the covers on my bed. The cool sheets feel glorious around my heated skin and I close my eyes praying that sleep doesn't elude me once again. It's been weeks upon months where I've not been able to sleep through the night. And though I'm one of the lucky few that doesn't need a lot of sleep to get by, the insomnia is starting to take its toll. My work hasn't suffered, not that I believe anyone besides Janice would notice, but the fear of falling asleep in a meeting or conference is a fear continually weighing on my shoulders. But even worse than falling asleep at work is the panic of it occurring while I watch Elle's kids. She doesn't ask me to babysit often, though I request it every chance that I get. I love those little nuggets, and when she does ask me they need my undivided attention.

Punching my pillow, I toss and turn for the next hour feeling no relief from my wakefulness.

"Ugh," I groan, finally giving into my brain's desire to be awake.

Trudging back into the kitchen, I start up my coffee machine, filling it to the brim, and flicking the television back on. Unfortunately for most people, at this hour all that seems to be playing are infomercials. But I grin inwardly. I love infomercials and seriously became an addict the first week I wasn't able to sleep, the dreams plaguing me of a time I'd rather forget. The infomercials gave me a way to turn my memories off and sink into something mindless.

The bubbling of the coffee machine and the aroma of the Brazilian beans I special order fill my space and I inhale deeply, relishing in the comfort of the scent. I stalk back into the kitchen and stare at the pot, silently begging it to fill up faster. When my pleas go unanswered, I shuffle back to my bedroom and remove my clothing, deciding that a quick shower to wash off the grime from the day before is in order, and it will keep my mind off of the sweet nectar brewing down the hall.

The warm spray feels like millions of tiny stings across my skin, the common aftermath when I've experienced this dream. The sinister gazes, the cold concrete, the pungent scent of sweat. It all brings back memories I'd rather forget. A time when I was reckless, wild, and careless. A time that has set me on my current path.

Under the spray, I take the time to wash my hair and shave every inch of my body. I've always believed in daily maintenance because one of my fears is being in some sort of accident and having to be rushed to the hospital and my clothes stripped away. I know it's self-absorbed, but I'd rather not look like a Sasquatch or a have full bush if that ever happens, thank you very much.

Turning off the water and wrapping a towel around my hair and then my body, I step out of the shower stall and grab my body lotion off the counter. Dropping the fabric knotted around my chest, I slather my body with the vanilla scented lotion until I'm so thoroughly greased up that I would sizzle on a frying pan.

I step into my bedroom, gathering a pair of gym shorts and a tank top from what I call my "casual at home attire" drawer in my dresser and reach into the drawer above to snag a bra and panties. In the darkness of my room, I don't even care if any of the clothing I've picked out matches, I plan on spending my day sifting through the files I've brought home. Tomorrow after I go to church with my mother and brother, I may see if Elle wants to take the kids to the park. I make it a point to do at least one thing outside of my home on the weekends.

Unraveling the towel from my hair I scrunch the strands between the material a few times to remove as much excess water as possible, then I spin on my heels and carry the towel back to my bathroom, hanging it and my body towel on the rod beside the shower to dry. Without glancing in the mirror, I grab a small bottle of leave-in conditioner from the counter around my sink. After applying it to my hair, I reach for my brush, running the bristles through the wet strands. I'm one of the lucky few that can get away with air-drying my hair without any of the frizz that people complain about. I actually prefer the soft waves left behind when I allow it to dry on its own.

A tune that I heard on the radio yesterday worms its way into my ear and I begin to hum along as I walk back to my kitchen, my eyes lighting up with joy at the sight of the full coffeepot.

"Come to momma," I say to the object as I reach into the cabinet to grab my favorite Minnie Mouse mug. I pour the brown liquid into the cup, add my cream and sugar, and then close my eyes in complete bliss as I take that first sip.

"God, yes. Who needs sex when I have you?" I whisper in ecstasy. I haven't had sex, well, good sex, in a few years, so my statement rings pretty damn true at the moment.

Taking a few more mouthfuls of the potent liquid, I walk back to my living room with a new bounce in my step and saddle up for the infomercials that I love. It doesn't take long before I've ordered an air fryer, a makeup set, and a pressure washer. I'm not even sure what I'd use the latter for, but it seemed like a good idea at the time. Thank goodness I'm not a hoarder.

Yet.

If this insomnia doesn't stop, then I'm probably going to have to get a bigger space to put all the shit that I've started to accumulate. Thank goodness my condo also comes with a garage, but mine just happens to be on the other side of the community. It's easier for me to just park in front of my place.

Blindly taking a sip from my mug, I groan when it comes up empty. Just as I'm about to stand from my couch a commercial from the local animal shelter comes on the television and I have to fight back the tears.

A dog. No, a cat. Wait, I don't want to be a spinster cat lady. I need a dog. That one with the cute lopsided ears.

I make a note to myself to go by the shelter tomorrow and get a pet. I'm not sure why I never considered getting one before. My hours at work are crazy, but perhaps a pet would give me an excuse to no longer work extra hours. Yes, I'm going to do it. I'm going to get a dog.

It's been three hours since I made my life-changing decision and I have a list a mile long of all the things I'll need to purchase to bring home a new pet. I've also finally started sorting through my work files.

The first stack I breeze through, they're pretty cut and dry with the terms and won't take much time to mediate.

The second stack is only a bit more difficult because there are children involved, something I always tackle from the get-go before I work on settling any of the other terms. Custody battles always bring out the worst in people, so I try my hardest to get it done as quickly and as cleanly as possible.

The last stack staring back at me consists of only one folder – the Cullan case. The wife is the one that reached out to Mr. Nemmer to represent her which he agreed to and then handed off to me, but I'm sure he still plans on seeing a hefty payout from the client. The Cullans happen to own one of the largest site development firms in our area. Normally splitting the business is a piece of cake, but this one gets tricky because Gemma, the wife, began working as a secretary to husband and slowly bought shares of the company before she and Sammy, the husband got married. They now co-own the business and her allotment of shares in the business is up for debate. So, after the dissolution of thirty years of marriage, not only do I get to deal with two people that have argued the past two times they have been in our practice, but I get to confront a business lawyer and possibly an accountant as well. Oh, and they also have two sets of twins, one set twenty-five and the other eleven, and a history of police calls of domestic violence, but neither party press charges when the police actually arrive.

I rub my forehead remembering the last time they were in the office meeting with Mr. Nemmer and Sammy's lawyer to fill out paperwork. The shouting had been at such a high level that our neighboring building had sent their security guard over believing that we had been attacked. Luckily, the guard was able to separate the duo and the paperwork was signed.

Tossing the file back onto the coffee table I slouch back against my couch and glance once more at the clock, noting the morning hour. I consider heading to the onsite gym or making breakfast, but it seems my stomach has made up my mind for me. Breakfast it is. I suppose the one good thing about not being able to sleep through the night is the amount of work I'm able to tackle before the rest of the world awakes.

Pulling out some ingredients, I crack a few eggs in a bowl and set aside some vegetables and cheese for the makings of an omelet. I giggle as my stomach rumbles loudly as I wait for my skillet to heat up. Carefully I pour the mixture into the pan just as my cell phone begins to ring.

"Shit," I grumble as I make a mad dash over to my living room to grab the phone, blindly swiping the button to talk to the caller. "Hello?"

"Hey," my best friend answers on the other line. "What are you doing right now?"

"Well," I begin, "I'm making some breakfast. What about you?" I ask as I test the edges of the omelet, seeing they are not quite the consistency I'm looking for.

"Jackson, stop," she murmurs, and I don't fight back the small grin that grows on the corner of my lips. "Sorry, do you think you could come by this morning?"

"Do you need me to watch the kids?"

"No, but I wanted to talk to you about something. And don't freak out. It's nothing bad."

It's incredible how well she knows me. My mind immediately went to a worst-case scenario.

"Okay, what time?"

"Well, Jackson was saying," she starts but a knock on my door draws my attention.

"Hey, let me call you back. Someone is at my door," I tell her as I end the call and rush to the entrance of my apartment. Without checking the peephole, I open the door and immediately wish I hadn't. Cooper, Jackson's incredibly handsome and arrogant brother, stands before me in a tight black T-shirt and jeans that hug his muscled thighs. I've never had a reaction to a man like I have to Cooper. Well, it has happened once before, but I'd rather not dwell on that mishap.

Cooper stands before me with his cocky grin and perfect blond hair just mussed enough to look like he rolled out of someone's bed after going at it all night long. His smile quickly falls as he peers over my shoulder.

"Something burning?"

"Huh?" I whisper, then I remember the breakfast I had been cooking when Elle called. "Oh, shit," I shout as I leave my door open and rush back to my kitchen. The smell of burnt egg leaves me gagging as I turn off the burner and remove the pan from the stove.

"Omelet?" a deep voice asks from over my shoulder, startling me, and I jump back with a hand on my heaving chest.

"Sorry," he apologizes.

Finally getting my bearings about me, I reply, "Yes, it was."

"I didn't know you wore glasses," he points out, and I remember that I still have my reading glasses perched on my nose.

Quickly removing them from my face, I tell him, "I don't. They're just for when I have to read a lot."

"Cute. I like them."

"Mmhmm," I murmur.

We stand in silence in my kitchen, our gazes locked on one another. I'm actually surprised to find that his eyes aren't traveling up and down my body. That seems to be the case most of the time I'm alone with a man. Jackson has been the only one up to this point that can have a conversation with me and not stare at my chest. Elle found herself a good one.

"Cooper," I begin, and he cocks one of those perfectly masculine brows upward. "What are you doing here?"

Chapter Two

Cooper

I STARE AT SARA, trying my best not to scan her body from the tips of her pink painted toes to the top of her wavy blonde head. If ever there was a woman that fit into my perfect mold – it would be Sara. But along with that beauty comes a sassy mouth and a fiery attitude. We haven't been around each other much, just a few occasions when Elle and my brother had invited us both over, but since I had moved into Jackson's home when he moved in with Elle, I had been seeing Sara in passing more and more.

I was actually taken aback when she opened her door. I hadn't been expecting her to be wearing gym shorts and a form-fitting tank, having never seen her in anything other than her business suits and the occasional jean shorts. But the glasses perched on her nose clinched my chest, and I was a goner. I had always loved a woman wearing glasses. They made her cerulean eyes even more alluring.

She had just asked me a question, but for the life of me I can't remember what she said outside of the muffled noises going on in my head.

"Uh, what?" I ask her to repeat her question.

She places two fists on her hips and, without fail, they draw my attention to the hourglass curve of her hips.

"Why are you here, Cooper?"

"Oh," I begin casually as I lean against her kitchen counter. "I was closing up a case this morning and Jackson asked me to come over. When I told him I was at the office, he told me to swing by and grab you. Kill two birds with one stone or something like that."

"Hmm. Do you know what it's about?" she questions as she takes the burnt mess in her frying pan and scraps it into the trash.

"Nope. Not a clue."

"I can drive myself, you know."

"Of course I know that," I bicker back at her. "But Elle and Jackson asked me to pick you up, so here I am."

With narrowed eyes, she turns her attention back to me as she steps over to her sink. "How did you know where I lived?"

"It isn't hard to figure out, Sara."

"Cop privileges?" she inquires with a bit of harshness that rubs me the wrong way.

"Detective," I remind her, proud of my recent promotion. "And, no. Anyone with internet can figure it out."

"Hmm. . . Well, isn't that a lovely thought."

"Come on. I'd like to get this over with so that I can get some rest. I've been up all night."

She rolls her eyes and continues to scrub the pan in her hand.

"Please, I'll even buy you breakfast."

It only takes a moment, but she drops the pan in the sink and motions for me to take over.

"Clean that up and I'll be right back." She moves around me and I catch the faint hint of vanilla as she sweeps past. "Oh, and I want waffles," Sara demands as she walks down the hall to what I assume is her bedroom, leaving me elbow deep in water and suds.

I manage to finish washing the pan for Sara, and after scrounging around her cabinets, I locate a Tupperware to put her chopped up vegetables into.

"Oh, you didn't have to do that. I was just joking," I vaguely hear her say but my eyes are trained on her long legs barely covered by tiny denim shorts. By her thighs, a pair of white converse sneakers dangles from her fingers. My gaze travels up to her shirt and I bite back a chuckle when I read the graphic on her shirt.

My life revolves around coffee, coffee, and more coffee.

"It's fine and now it's all done." Sara nods her head as she places her sneakers on the barstool beside where she stands. "Cute shirt," I mention and she glances down as if forgetting what shirt she put on.

"Thanks."

At this point, Sara and I have known each other for a little less than a year, and all I know about her is that she is a divorce lawyer and Elle's best friend. We tend to bicker when we're together or she's off chasing Elle's kids around. It makes me wonder why she's still single. No one can deny how absolutely gorgeous she is and the fact that she has to be brilliant to be a lawyer obviously doesn't go unnoticed. Maybe she has some weird fetish or habit that I'm unaware of.

"Ready? You know it's silly for you to drive since you live next door to them. I can drive separately."

"I'm just following orders, and I think Elle has plans for you both today. Jackson said they'd bring you back."

"Whatever, this is silly." She stomps down the hall after closing and locking her door. I follow behind her, my gaze never leaving the sweet curve of her ass as she takes each step. As we approach my car I can hear her mumble beneath her breath, "It's like they forget I'm an adult. Let alone a grown woman that can take care of herself."

"No one will argue with you there," I say appreciatively, earning me a glare that pins me in place.

"I'm only going with you because you owe me breakfast."

"Yes, ma'am," I reply, opening the passenger side door and noticing Sara's eyes lift in surprise at the gesture. Chivalry may be dead to some, but definitely not for me. My mother would tan my hide if she knew I didn't open the door for a woman.

"Thanks."

In the car, I pull away from the condo complex and head toward my favorite diner off the beaten path. I've lived here most of my life except for the few months I was in the police academy and this place has always served the best breakfasts. It's a place my father used to take Jackson and me every Saturday when we were younger, claiming he wanted to let my mother catch a few extra hours of sleep.

We ride in silence and it follows us as we enter the diner and the waitress tells us to grab a seat anywhere. With my hand gently placed on Sara's back, I guide us toward a booth toward the other end of the diner, the same booth my father likes to frequent.

True to her word, Sara orders a stack of waffles without even glancing at her menu while I order the sausage, biscuits, and gravy skillet meal.

"How can you eat that and stay in such good shape?" Sara asks.

"Admiring?" I reply.

"Geez, cocky much?"

"Want to find out how cocky I really am? And I could say the same about you too."

"What, that I'm cocky?"

"No, that you're ordering a plate of carbs and sugar. Not sure those are on any healthy eating lists."

"Oh." She shrugs as she looks down at the cracked table, one of her small fingers reaching out to trace along the fracture.

The rest of our breakfast is eaten in silence, and it's awkward as hell. I'm usually good with holding conversations with people, getting them to speak to me. It's part of what makes me a good detective. But with Sara, my talents are suppressed.

"Hey, I'm sorry if I said something to upset you," I point out as I pay the bill, inwardly considering that I may have hurt her feelings earlier.

"You didn't." Sara doesn't look up from her phone as she responds, her face marred with wrinkles as she hastily types out a message.

"Telling Elle that I've already pissed you off today? That has to be a new record. It usually takes me a few hours."

Finally, she gazes up from her phone in surprise.

"What? No, I. . .um. . .have a difficult client that was handed to me yesterday and I was messaging my boss asking why."

"Why is it difficult?" I say as I rest back against the booth seat intrigued and ready to hear more. I always thought that being a divorce lawyer would be boring and mundane, if not sad. Watching and helping people split apart their lives.

"I can't really talk much about it – client confidentiality. It's just that it was a case originally given to my superior and he's a jackass that decided to hand it off because he'd rather go golfing."

"Does that happen a lot?"

"More frequently since I became a senior partner. Everyone is handing their work off to me it seems."

I watch her eyes as she speaks and I can see the unhappiness dripping inside them, the hollowness that she feels with each passing day.

"Do you like your job?"

"It pays the bills." She smirks as she rolls her eyes.

"That's not what I asked."

"I know."

Before I have a chance to question her further the waitress returns my card and I usher Sara from the restaurant and back to my car.

We're halfway on our way to Elle's house when the silence becomes too much for me. Sara must have the same thought because as I reach over to turn up the volume on the radio, our fingers brush against each other. A spark of awareness travels up my arm spurring a tingling sensation just behind my ear.

"Sorry," she whispers and turns back to face the window, but not before I notice the color on her skin drain away. Not typically the reaction I get when I touch a woman's body. Usually, it's a blush of pink followed by a heated gaze of longing and invitation.

"Any kind of music you prefer?" I ask her as the sounds of a rock band flow from the speakers filling the car with a heavy guitar riff.

"No, this is fine," Sara says absently.

"Hmm. . ."

My neighborhood comes into view and I turn down the main road leading to my house which neighbors Elle's. The exterior was in shambles when she moved in, but we've all chipped in to help fix it up. Which reminds me of something.

"I haven't seen your brother around. Is he still working for Jackson?"

"I think he's disappointed Elle is no longer single and yeah, he loves working at the landscaping business. I think Jackson mentioned bringing him on at the gym too."

Recently I haven't been able to help my brother and cousin run our landscaping company, my hours have been unpredictable at most, so they've had to start taking on more employees to pick up the slack. The business has been booming which has put a nice cushion in my back pocket.

The manicured lawns blur into one as I travel down the road and pull into the driveway I share with Elle. The driveway that caused a lot of tension when she first moved in, so I made it a point to expand it the first day I was in the house. Now we no longer have to rearrange vehicles just to leave. This means none of my late night guests have to worry about being blocked in after I've pissed them off by kicking them out after an evening of sex.

Removing the keys from the ignition, I look over to Sara and find her still staring out the window lost in her own world.

"Hey, you okay?" I ask her, sensing a bit of vulnerability I've never witnessed from her before. She's always seemed so strong and resilient, if not a bit snooty and full of herself. She's what I call a princess when I speak about her to Jackson.

I remember the first time I saw her with Elle at a local steakhouse for lunch. Her blonde hair pulled tightly against her face reminded me of my fourth-grade teacher, the first woman to give me a hard-on. She was a mix between a naughty librarian with the way her suit hugged her body like a second skin and a military officer with the stern look and vibe she was giving off. But I couldn't help myself from focusing my gaze on her – until Jackson groaned as we walked past noticing his new neighbor. He bickered the entire lunch about how this sprite of a woman was single-handedly destroying his life, but I was too busy trying to remember why she seemed so familiar, like we had met before.

"Yeah," she sighs bringing me back into the moment.

We exit the car and head up the concrete path toward the front door. Before we have a chance to knock or ring the doorbell the door swings open and two sets of big brown eyes gaze up at us in excitement and mischief.

"Kids, what did I tell you about opening the door? What if that was a stranger?" I hear Elle shout from the kitchen and the smiles on the kids' faces dim just a smidge.

"But it was Auntie Sara and Uncle Cooper. I sawed them pull up!" the little girl, Kennedy, shouts.

But I can't focus on the ringing in my ear from her high-pitched wail, it's the light twinkle of a giggle coming from Sara that draws my attention.

Elle finally steps out from her kitchen to greet us and says that Jackson will be right out and she offers us some croissants she had made this morning. If there was ever a reason to move into my brother's home, it's to have the pleasure of grabbing Elle's baked goods on a daily basis. Hell, if my brother and her ever end things I plan on breaking the bro code and going after her, if only for her baking skills.

A moan escapes my lips as I taste the buttery goodness melt in my mouth.

"That good?" Elle asks, chewing her bottom lip in nervousness. "It's a new recipe."

"Mmm, so good," I groan and look over at Sara, winking in her direction. Instead of blushing like I expected she rolls her eyes and reaches down to take Kennedy in her arms as the little boy, Noah, wraps himself around her leg.

"So, what's this news? Are you knocked up?" I ask jokingly, and I practically choke on the doughy goodness in my mouth when Elle's eyes double in size.

"Cooper," Sara chastises. "Don't be crude."

"What? It's a legitimate question."

"No, it's idiotic," Sara returns and leaves the room with Kennedy in her arms and Noah trailing behind.

My gaze travels back to Elle and she seems to have composed herself if her warm grin is any indication.

"We'll share the news when Jackson joins us. He was just taking a quick shower."

I nod silently and take a seat at one of the barstools at the kitchen island as Elle begins to pull out various ingredients for some muffins she's to deliver tomorrow. Absentmindedly I grab a piece of paper from her counter and begin making various folds in the sheet, practicing something that I picked up from an ex-girlfriend.

"Oh, is that a swan?" Sara asks from behind me just as my brother steps into the room, his hair still wet from his shower.

"Yeah, my ex taught me some origami. It's a good stress reliever," I reply to her question as Jackson presses a kiss to the top of Elle's head.

"So?" Sara prods anxiously.

My brother, being the asshole that he is, looks at us like we've grown two heads and asks Sara what she's talking about.

"So, what?"

Speaking up, I leave the paper swan on the table and stare at my brother in anger.

"Look, man, I've been up for twenty-seven hours. You called and asked us to come over. So, please, for the love of all that is Holy, tell us whatever secret it is you're harboring so that I can get some sleep."

My brother stares down at the woman that stole his heart and I can already sense what they plan on telling us. I don't even try to fight the grin that grows on my lips, but it's the downturn of Sara's lips that I notice in my peripheral.

"We're engaged!" Elle shouts in excitement, her tiny body bouncing on the tips of her toes.

"What?" Sara gasps in surprise as if she didn't expect this to happen, and it immediately draws my wary eye.

Elle rushes over to Sara and wraps her arms around her best friend. "Yeah, it happened a few days ago. And I'm sorry we didn't say anything sooner, but we kind of wanted to bask in the newness without the kids around. Are you mad?"

"I'm just surprised," Sara says as she weakly smiles down at her friend. Her reaction wipes the smile from my face and I stare at her in confusion, but she never meets my gaze.

"Well, there is one more thing I, well, we, wanted to talk to you about. Both of you," Elle says, her attention turning over toward me.

She drags Sara toward their living room, practically pushing her onto the couch and I follow suit.

"So. . ." I egg on, noticing for the first time the nervousness across Elle's features, but she smiles as her children situate themselves on Sara's lap.

"You know my busy season is about to start, especially since I branched out to wedding cakes and things like that, and Jackson will be working overtime with the landscaping business for the summer. But we want to get married as soon as possible. So, we were hoping that maybe you both could take over the planning of the wedding for us," she says in one breath.

Elle must have taken note of the confusion on my face because she worries her lip and gazes up at Jackson who lovingly grabs her hand. She knows how demanding my job can be, and I'm sure Sara's is the same. Even though most of my demands are self-enforced. I just don't have anything better to do with my time.

"I know what you both must be thinking, but we're hiring an event planner. We just need someone to meet with her and make decisions. We know the basics of what we want, but there aren't two other people that know us any better than you two. It would mainly be on the weekends, which is when we're tied up the majority of the time."

"I'm not sure if you've noticed, but we haven't really spent a lot of time together, and the few times we have it hasn't been all sunshine and rainbows."

"Please, guys. It would mean the world to us and will take some of the stress off our backs."

I consider their request, only for a moment, because never in my life has my younger brother ever asked me for anything. He has always been the most resilient of our bunch, the one that was hard-headed enough to achieve any goal he set forth.

Before I have a chance to accept Sara is running her fingers through her hair in exasperation, which confuses both myself, and if Elle's face is any indication, her as well.

"I'm so busy with everything right now, Elle. It's just not a good time for me. Work is crazy busy and. . .I mean. . .can't you guys wait a little bit or something? What's the rush?"

Without a second thought, I grab Sara's arm and yank her out of the room, through the sliding glass doors, and deposit her onto their porch with more force than is probably necessary.

"What the hell is your problem?" I shout at her.

"My problem? You should ask them what the hell they're thinking."

"Seriously? Cynical much?"

"Cynical? I'm a fucking divorce lawyer, the same one that handled Elle's divorce. Do you have any idea how many marriages end in divorce? Half, Cooper. Half. I can't believe she wants to go through with this again. It was a nightmare last time."

"Do you hear yourself? Do you have any idea how ridiculous you sound right now? Your best friend is asking you to support her for her big day. A day that is going to be the happiest day of her life. So as much as you may hate her decision, she is excited, and you bet your ass that you're going to march back in that room and apologize to them," I scold her like a child. I never would have imagined her outburst at their engagement announcement. I had an inkling that her fear of Elle getting hurt would play a part if an engagement ever occurred, but never something of this magnitude. She claims her job is the reason she's so jaded toward marriage, but I wonder if there is something more, something she isn't telling me.

She crosses her arms across her chest, pushing her breasts up and drawing my eyes. "What happens if I don't?"

"I'll cuff you and drag you in there myself. And you better believe that I have ways to make you talk."

"You're bluffing," she teases as she takes a step toward me. I can smell the sweet vanilla of her perfume or lotion, and I have to fight back the groan threatening to escape.

Mimicking her movement, I take a step toward her, my chest brushing against her arms. "Try me," I threaten and she narrows her eyes at me before turning around and stomping back into the house.

I give her a moment to apologize without my interference before I decide to stroll back into the house. My brother stands in the kitchen, his arms crossed against his body as he watches the girls interact. Without looking in my direction, I hear him thank me for speaking with Sara.

"I'm going to head home and get some sleep," I tell Jackson as I head toward the front door, only to be stopped by Elle on my way out asking where I'm headed.

"But, I need to go over with you the specifics of what we need," she frets.

The headache that has been slowly building behind my eyes starts to pound heavily.

"Look, Elle-" I begin, but I'm interrupted as Jackson comes back into the space and explains to Elle that Sara can relay the information to me.

"Yeah, I'll stop by Sara's tomorrow and we can get started."

"I have plans," Sara informs us with a grunt.

"No, you don't," I argue.

"Yes, I do," the woman practically stomps with her reply which only causes me to roll my eyes at her antics.

"No, you really don't. You're probably going to sit in your apartment and work all day."

Elle tries to butt into the conversation, but with Sara standing only a few inches from me, neither of us breaks our heated stare. I watch as the edge of Sara's nose flares with every puff of air she takes, her anger cultivating like a cloud around us.

It's Jackson that finally cut through the tension.

"I'm not sure if they're going to fuck or throw punches."

Taking a step back, I make a hasty exit toward the door, not wanting anyone to notice the significant tent in my pants. Who knew that getting a rise out of Sara would be such a turn on?

As I step across the threshold, I shout out a reminder about tomorrow and adjust my pants all the way back to my home, not wanting to give Ms. Stephens a fright, or thrill, as she walks to her mailbox across the street.

Inside my home, I hastily retreat to my bedroom and remove all of my clothing, loving that my dog barely pays me any mind as she snoozes on her dog bed in the corner of my room. Jackson must have let her out this morning; otherwise she'd be pawing at my legs to be let outside.

Groaning I fall back on my bed, my muscles aching from the strenuous work out I put them through after my shift, but it's my cock still standing high and mighty that has my attention.

"Why her?" I ask myself out loud actually expecting an answer from anyone. I squeeze my eyes shut tightly. Praying that my cock gets its head on straight, but once my eyes close it's clouded by visions of soft blonde hair and tanned skin.

"Gah!" I grunt. I consider hopping into a cold shower to have the chill take care of this predicament I've found myself in, but I've never been a fan of the cold water method. Instead, I take matters into my own hands and find my release as I playback my argument with Sara from moments before. It only takes a few minutes, quicker than any I've ever had, and when I'm done cleaning myself up, I'm finally able to drift off to sleep.

Only to dream of a reckless night with a stunning blonde.

Chapter Three

Sara

"SO, WHAT WAS THAT about?" Elle asks from behind me as I turn and stare at Cooper's retreating back, admiring the way his muscles ripple under his tight T-shirt. Damn that man for being so delectable and ornery at the same time, he makes my head spin.

"What are you talking about?" I turn back toward my best friend noting the happiness seeping from her body. I can't believe I questioned her desire to get married again. I know that I'm jaded, but I have my reasons, and I'm lucky enough that Elle understands them.

"You guys were giving off some major heat."

"You're delusional."

"I'm just saying. I saw what I saw."

"What you saw was a man trying to dictate my actions. You know how I feel about that."

"Mmhmm," she says with a dreamy far off look in her eyes causing me to narrow mine in her direction. "Sometimes being dictated by a man isn't so bad."

And now I understand her look.

"Ew."

Of course, I can't say I wouldn't let Jackson dictate me in the bedroom either. My best friend has a certified hottie at her beck and call. And his brother is just as hot, probably even more with his dark blond hair and tattoos that barely peek out from his work clothes. I only know about them because I was stunned speechless during one of the dinners Elle hosted and he got food on his shirt. We were all blessed with the vision of his bare chest when he removed the shirt and grabbed one of Jackson's. A few of Elle's friends and I actually groaned when he covered himself up once more.

"Don't be jealous that I'm getting laid."

Damn her.

"You're probably right. It's been so freaking long."

"What happened to the last guy. Tom? Or something like that."

"Tim," I correct. "And I got bored," I say with a shrug. "Come on. I really do have work to do this weekend, and if I am going to have time to spare when the asshole stops by tomorrow, I should probably get started."

"You work too much."

"And you've just added more to my plate."

I mean it jokingly, but I can see the hurt in Elle's face as I remind her how busy I am. But I realize that her business is booming, so much so she's looking to hire some help and buy a bigger space.

Reaching out I take one of her hands in mine. "You know I am honored to help you, Elle. You're my best friend and I never got to be a part of this with your first wedding."

"That's because Dan was a jerk."

"Certifiable."

We take a seat on the couch against the wall and Elle grabs a notebook from the coffee table then hands it to me. She shows me the clips of magazines, rough edges of paper torn directly from their place and I stare at the collage of photos feeling an overwhelming sense of apprehension. My hand trembles as I flip one of the pages and take in the visions of cakes and linens.

"Uh, Elle, are you sure that I'm the right person to do this? You know how I feel about weddings."

With a giggle, my friend closes the book and places it on her lap. "What? Afraid you'll break out in hives again."

"Hey, that only happened one time! And I'm pretty sure it was from something I ate."

"No, you're just allergic to commitment. I mean, even us talking about it has your neck and chest turning splotchy," Elle points out, and I subconsciously reach up and scratch the point where my neck meets my shoulder. "Maybe. . .you should take the same advice you gave me last year and put yourself out there. What do you have to lose, Sara?"

"Uh, I could become a neurotic nutjob like my mother did when my father left her. Or a conniving bitch. Or a heartbroken spinster that replaces her heart with forty cats. Take your pick. I see this every day, Elle. I'm not cut out for relationships."

"But you are!" she argues, the sound of her voice drawing her two angels from their rooms where they timely crawl onto my lap. I take a deep breath, inhaling their sweet smell of innocence. "What do you call our friendship?"

Settling the kids on my lap, I lean my head against her daughter Kennedy's and smile. "A sisterhood."

"No, we're best friends. That's a relationship. Now, go find yourself a date or an escort, or something, or I'm going to do it for you."

My eyes widen at her threat. Elle's never been known for her matchmaking skills, her first husband is a prime example. "You wouldn't dare."

"Try me."

Even with her precious kids in my lap, her notebook beckons my gaze, and I feel my heart speed up at the thought of having to plan Elle's special day.

"Hey, before you freak out, which I can see clearly all over your face, we've hired an event planner. You and Cooper need to schedule a meeting with her. She's going to plan everything, you and Cooper will pretty much be stand-ins for us. That's all. You know how busy my business gets in the spring and summer and I know how busy you both are."

And I do. Elle lives and breathes her baking business from March through September. And now that she's taken on wedding cakes as well, I'm not sure how she finds time to sleep.

The next few hours are spent playing with her kids on the gaming system attached to the television, and a few rounds where I kick Jackson's ass in Mario Kart and Duck Hunt. I'll never tell him that I love that they have all of the old gaming systems – I'm a bit of a gamer girl.

Back at my condo, I take in the large living room that now seems far too empty. Earlier when Cooper filled the space it felt – different, warm. Now the white walls seem cold and clinical against my neutral furniture. I've never been inside Cooper's house, but I'm guessing it's dark and full of leather. Your typical bachelor pad. Which has me wondering why Cooper is still single. He has a great job and no one would argue that he's stunningly attractive – enough to make me do a double take when he walks past. And I know I'm not alone when my panties melt at his saucy grin. It's one of the features that make me hate him more.

Is it possible to hate someone because you're attracted to them? But somewhere, I feel like I've felt this same rippling sensation I get when he's near before.

Staring at the stack of files still placed in a precarious position on my coffee table, I consider spending some time delving into them again, but instead I walk past the impending doom of paper waiting for my review and stroll toward my kitchen to grab my car keys and decide to head toward my happy place – Target.

The cart I push through the aisles is filled to the brim, and I'm not even sure what I've put inside. It started with a few shirts I saw in the clothing section, a pair of sandals that I just had to have, and then once I reached the toy department all of my self-control evaporated into thin air. I love buying toys for Elle's kids, especially because I watch them at my place as often as I can. I passed homeware a few aisles back and decided I needed some new plates, towels, and sheets. Now I'm lost in a field of cookware wondering if I need another Crock-Pot when I feel him before I see him.

"I'd go for the cast iron if it was me."

My back stiffens as his arms reach around to the cart handles cradling me against his muscled body. The scent of his cologne assaults my senses, and I bite back the urge to take a deep inhale and have it penetrate my lungs.

"What are you doing here?" I whisper, my voice sounding unfamiliar and husky even to my own ears.

"Same as you – shopping."

Fighting back the desire to turn around in his arms or rest my back against his chest, I squeeze my eyes tightly and say on a deep breath, "I thought you needed to sleep."

"Work decided differently. As did fate."

Cocking my head and tilting it to the side, I look back at Cooper in confusion. "Fate?"

"Sure, if work hadn't called me in to investigate some new evidence on a case and also grab some supplies for the office, I wouldn't have had the pleasure of running into you."

"Hmm. . .how did you find me by the way?"

"I was looking at the coffee makers. And make no mistake, I'll always recognize you."

The heat builds across my chest and crawls its way up my neck toward my cheeks. Even with my naturally tanned skin, my ruddy blush is always identifiable to the passing eye.

"What brings you here?" he asks and then slants his body to look toward my cart. "Except for maybe to buy the entire store."

"Shut up. I came to get some notebooks for Elle's wedding. I like to organize. And don't make fun of me. I walk into Target and then five hours later I find myself at home with items I don't remember purchasing. It's a hypnotic disease, I swear to you."

"You probably should have your head examined. It could be contagious."

Finally turning around to face Cooper I try not to frown when he drops his arms, but he doesn't step away, which leaves us within inches of each other. I'm not complaining.

"You're probably right. We probably both need to be admitted."

Nodding his head in agreement, he strikes his hand through his messy hair, and I audibly hear every woman within a fifteen-mile radius swoon.

"No one else I'd rather be quarantined with."

"If I didn't know better, Cooper, it sounds like you almost like me."

"Eh, things can change. . ." he begins until a woman turns the corner and screeches so loudly that a ringing persists in my ear as she grabs his arm to bring his attention toward her before wrapping herself around his body.

Watching their exchange, I can't help but roll my eyes as I turn back around and grip the handles of the cart. I push away and walk toward the office supplies without a second glance behind me, but I can feel his stare, and it burns through my clothes and skin, embedding itself deep within the muscles and tissue. Damn him for making me feel anything other than the life I've been given. Jealousy isn't something I'm foreign to, but I steer clear of it whenever possible. Hence another reason I stay away from relationships.

But while I'm here, I wonder if Target sells vibrators.

In the middle of my bed, I sit surrounded by a mountain of plastic bags filled with items that could be deemed as necessary or not, depending on which minute you ask me. Regardless, I blame my shopping excursion on Cooper. I had my few purchases under control, but once I saw that gorgeous woman wrap her arms around the man that made my anger boil and simultaneously stomach clench at the same time, I couldn't stop shopping.

Feeling like I made a big mistake at the shopping center, I kick my legs, and all of the bags and articles scatter on the rug on the floor beneath my bed. All I can think is that Cooper is the reason why I did this and with a heavy sigh, I fall back onto my bed and stare up at my boring white ceiling. I hate this feeling, this fear of the rug being pulled out from under me. That's what jealousy feels like to me, this vice worming its way through my blood and infecting everything inside of my body. And I'm absolutely jealous over someone that isn't even mine.

"Stop being an idiot, Sara," I tell myself and then after a deep breath, I jump from the bed, clean up the mess I've made on the floor, and order some dinner.

Luckily the Chinese restaurant I love is only a few blocks away so it doesn't take long until the delicious aroma fills my place. I ignore the stack of work on my coffee table and prop my feet up with my plate resting on my legs as I binge on a reality TV marathon.

A few episodes in and my plate long ago cleared, I'm captivated by the two girls clawing at each other on the screen. I barely notice that the sun has completely set and I sit in the darkness, the only light coming from the television screen and a small night-light plugged in the outlet in the hallway behind me. A knock sounds on my door, and I startle so much that my plate and fork clatter on my hardwood floor.

"Crap," I murmur as I pick up the mess and wonder who would be at my place this time of night. Before I answer the door I take in the time – 10:07 p.m. I bite the edge of my lip wondering if I should ignore the person on the other side of my door and I've almost reached that conclusion until another round of pounding begins.

I stand on my tiptoes to gaze out of the peephole and I stifle a groan as I pull the door open.

"What are you doing here?"

"Can't a guy just come by and say hello?"

"No."

Cooper stands before me, just as handsome as he was in Target earlier, and my heart begins to throb wildly. Stupid organ. Without an invitation Cooper brushes past me and into my living room, leaving me standing at the doorway wondering why the man can't seem to take no for an answer.

"Did you need something?" I ask him as he stands in the middle of the room, the space seeming much smaller, watching the women fight on the screen. He seems so entranced that he startles when I call his name, "Cooper?"

"Yes, sorry. I just remember that I need to be here with you tomorrow to start going over things and it just seemed silly for me to go home and come right back in the morning."

"So, you just what? Decided to come here tonight instead?"

"Pretty much. You have a couch, I'll just crash for the night."

"Shouldn't you ask me first?"

"Probably," he replies with a cocky grin as he takes a seat on my couch and reaches for the remote.

"Maybe I have company."

"You don't."

"How do you know?" I inquire, my voice rising at the same time my stomach begins to flutter as he takes off his shirt.

"Detective," He points out, as if I missed his job title announcement this morning. "Hey, do you mind if I grab some leftovers? I smell Chinese and I haven't eaten."

My mouth opens and closes like a guppy's as he moves from the couch and heads into my kitchen, opening the fridge and helping himself to a bottle of water and a container of food. I watch stunned, and in awe, as he tugs open drawers until he finds the utensils and then promptly leans against my counter and shovels the food into his mouth.

"Why is it so dark in here?" he asks around a mouthful of food bringing me out of my stupor.

"Because I was watching TV."

"Mmhmm."

"I'm sorry, but I've known you for almost a year now and all of a sudden you see yourself fit to pop into my place all willy-nilly, take off your shirt, and help yourself to my food and couch?"

"Willy-nilly?" he looks at me in confusion. At my answering growl, he goes back to helping himself to my leftovers. "So, which part are you madder about? That I took off my shirt or that I'm eating your food."

"All of it!" I shout, throwing my arms in the air. Though I pray my outburst doesn't cause him to put his shirt back on. I'm not opposed to the view that has been bestowed upon me. "You know what? I'm too tired to deal with this. If you're not going to leave, which you've so stubbornly proved, then please clean up after yourself. I'm going to bed. There are extra blankets and pillows in the hall closet."

In a hushed tone barely audible to my own ears, I hear Cooper mumble his thanks as I turn to double check the locks on my front door and head toward my bedroom. Just as I'm about to slam my bedroom door, I come to a dead halt and turn to look back down the hallway, barely able to make out Cooper in the kitchen.

Am I an idiot? He could be a killer. You can't trust anyone anymore.

But even though I stand in between the space separating my bedroom from the hallway I know that I already have an answer to my internal musings. It's not that he is Jackson's brother, or that he's a detective. It's that I feel an odd sense of comfort around Cooper, a protectiveness that is new yet familiar at the same time.

A memory from long ago tries to push its way forward but fades just as quickly.

"Goodnight, Cooper."

"G'night, Sara."

The clock continues to count the minutes away as I toss and turn throughout the night, my body reacting to the man sleeping on the other side of my condo on the couch. It's not until the early hours of the morning that I'm finally able to catch some sleep, but it's overflowing with visions of Cooper, his hands, his lips, and what I can only imagine as his impressive cock.

In the haze of the early morning, I release a heavy sigh as the man starring in my dream slides his hand down the back of my leg. I can practically feel the warmth of his palm as his thumb rubs a circle on my calf muscle. Then suddenly he's gripping my ankle and yanking me from both my dream and my bed.

"What the hell?" I ask, now realizing that the dream I was having was, in fact, Cooper in real life stroking my leg. My very exposed leg. "Why would you do that? And how did you get in here? I locked the door."

I struggle to regain my composure as I turn over and yank down the oversized T-shirt that I sleep in from where it's gathered under my arms, thankful that my breasts are still covered. My panties? Well, Cooper now has gotten an eyeful of the yellow cotton briefs with small white flowers speckles all over. Serves him right.

"I pegged you as more of a silk and lace kind of girl," Cooper points out as he tucks his hands into his jean pockets. Unfortunately, he has put his shirt back on covering up those delicious muscles and tattoos I want to appreciate.

Remembering that I'm braless under the thin shirt I cross my arms over my chest, not even caring that my hair is probably twisted up like a bird's nest or that I most likely have black smudges under my eyes.

"Are you going to answer me?"

"Which question would you like answered first?"

"Gosh, do you always have to be so aggravating?"

"Yes, it's fun to get a rise out of you. All I had to do was jiggle the knob to get the lock to pop open. And we need to get started because I have to go spend time with Bailey."

Ah, that must be the girl from yesterday.

"You could have just knocked on the door."

"My way was more fun."

"Whatever, get out so I can change."

He rolls his eyes and leaves my room, thankfully closing the door behind himself. I lean over to check my clock on the nightstand, groaning when it reads 6 a.m. I've only been asleep for three hours. It's going to be a long day.

After a quick shower and change of clothes, I leave my bedroom to find Cooper at my stove cooking eggs. His back is to me and I can't help but lick my lips as the muscles of his broad back ripple beneath his shirt as he moves the spatula against the pan.

"I made you some breakfast," Cooper says without turning around. I'm glad I wasn't caught ogling him.

He plates the food as I go to the living room and grab the notebook Elle gave me yesterday. If he's so determined to get this started, I hope to get some sort of plan ready as soon as possible so that I can get him out of my place. Even though the thought of him leaving causes an ache to grow in the pit of my stomach.

Taking a seat on the stool beside me, I try my hardest not to moan when the smell of his cologne wafts past my nose. Only Cooper would be able to sleep on the couch and still manage to smell delectable.

Pointing with his fork, Cooper gestures toward the notebook and asks, "What's that?"

"This is our mission, should you choose to accept it," I joke, but as usual, he comes back with a witty response.

"I am. The question is, are you?"

And for some reason, I'm not one hundred percent sure he's talking about the wedding as we lock eyes.

Am I?

Chapter Four

Cooper

BAILEY'S SOFT FUR SLIPS between my fingers as I stroke her back while she lounges beside me on the couch. Earlier today I spoke with the Captain about the scheduling issue we've been having in the department, offering a new set up as we bring on some new recruits and detectives. She was concerned that I was being stretched too thin, which is true, and more liable for mistakes. I agreed with her whole-heartedly. With the new schedule I suggested, I would have no trouble juggling Jackson's wedding. Now if only I could get Sara to cut back on her workload. Though I fear that she is trying to prove herself at her office in the male-dominated practice.

Tonight Sara and I are scheduled to meet the event planner at a local restaurant to go over the plans that Jackson and Elle had already discussed and come up with some sort of timeline when we would need to be available.

Knowing that the time has been slipping away while I focused on a baseball game playing on the television, I resign myself to go to the meeting to talk about flowers and lace. On the plus side, I'll get a decent meal out of it.

Enjoying the warm weather as I step from the house, I head toward the tarp covered mass in my driveway and pull it aside to reveal the motorcycle I don't get to ride as frequently as I'd like. Adjusting my helmet, I swing one of my legs over the seat and start the engine, the purr and vibrations earning a smile in return. Knocking the kickstand back, I wave at Jackson as he pulls into his driveway and make my way toward downtown.

The event planner suggested a restaurant located in the lower level of an old warehouse. The exposed brick and beams from decades ago give this place a modern and urban feel while still capturing the aspects of an historic building. As I take a step through the entrance, I can't help but appreciate the work before me. I've always been a sucker for historic buildings.

But the brick and mortar only hold my attention for so long. Without having to search the intimate room my eyes immediately lock onto the soft wavy hair that I instantly recognize as Sara's. I've always been mesmerized by the yellow and brown shades that weave themselves through the soft and silky strands, knowing that it's something many women pay hundreds of dollars for, but I'm certain Sara has been blessed with naturally.

As I bypass the hostess, much to her dismay if her scowl is any indication, I weave through the scattered tables and approach the booth. The pixie-like woman with short dark, almost black hair notices me first, a wide smile growing across her innocent face. The woman looks no older than a fifteen-year-old playing dress up, but when she stands to shake my hand, I'm surprised at the firm grip she returns. She introduces herself as Taylor and then presents the event planner Elle has hired as Kerry. The woman looks familiar, regal in her stance, and if I were in any other state of mind, I'd instantly be attracted to her. The long waves of dark red hair end at her waist and her bright blue eyes sparkle with a knowledge of which I'm not aware. Her pants and silk blouse don't hug her body, but beneath them her obvious curvy figure is apparent. Any other day I would be enthralled by the beautiful woman, but my attention, and cock, only have their eyes on the woman scowling in my direction.

"Thank you for joining us today, Mr. Divers," Kerry says as her introduction before gesturing for me to take a seat beside Sara, much to the chagrin of my bench mate.

"Cooper, please. I'm happy to be here to help. Anything for my brother."

"I wish more men were in involved in the planning. We aim to make it the most enjoyable of days not just for the bride, but for the groom as well. But first, let's order and enjoy dinner, then we can delve into business, shall we?" Kerry states matter-of-factly, a trait I can admire because most of the women I've dated in the past want me to steer the conversations and make choices for them. It's appealing to see a woman in command. It's probably another reason why I'm fascinated by the woman who has been inching closer to the wall since I've sat down.

As the waitress approaches I glance around the room and notice everyone dressed nicely, collared shirts and dresses adorn the men and women seated at their tables, while I sit here wearing my leather jacket, jeans, and riding boots. Not that I believe that they'd kick me out of the establishment, but I probably should have taken my attire into account before I left the house. And for the first time in a very *very* long time I feel out of place with the foreboding notion of being embarrassed. I barely notice that the server's eyes appreciatively run over my body or that she pays no mind to the three women sitting at the table, she's too busy vying for my attention. Finally, after ordering a bottle of wine for the table, does she leave with the corner of her lips tilted up in a seductive grin that I have zero interest in pursuing.

The two women across from me begin conversing to each other while I focus on the menu placed before me at the table, the words barely registering as I fight against this unfamiliar emotion. It's not until I feel a warmth seeping through my leather jacket do I look over to find Sara's hand resting on my arm. Since I've arrived, it's the first time she's acknowledged my presence.

"Are you okay?"

I fight the urge to lie and tell her everything is fine just so we can move onto something else, but with the way her eyes lock onto mine, I find myself telling her the truth.

Holding the lapel of my jacket, I point out, "I probably should have reconsidered my attire tonight." My quick chuckle isn't returned by Sara as she narrows her eyes at me, but I can see when recognition dawns. Her entire face relaxes and she smiles with a warmth I've only ever witnessed from my mother.

"You feel out of place. I'm sorry; I didn't even consider the restaurant choice when we agreed to the meeting."

Not wanting Sara to feel an ounce of shame I rest my hand on top of hers, struggling to ignore the awareness that travels from the tips of my fingers up to my shoulder. I don't reply with words. Instead, I squeeze her hand gently and let her know that it's okay.

She doesn't move her hand from under mine, both of us seem to enjoy the feeling of the other's touch. The familiarity of the hold.

"Why don't you take off your jacket and stay awhile?" she jokes and for the first time since I arrived I find myself returning her grin.

"I'm only wearing a T-shirt underneath. I'm not sure they'd approve of the tattoos and short sleeves."

"I think that you're a paying customer and they shouldn't judge you based on your attire and what you look like."

She seems so adamant that before I even realize it, she's helping me remove my jacket and placing it on the edge of the booth between her and the wall. Which now that I think about it was a genius move because now it forces her to sit closer to me.

"All of the waitstaff collectively swooned. Men and women. They won't be kicking you out."

Looking toward the kitchen area and watching the staff scatter about, a few brave souls wink in my direction.

"But the question is, Sara, did you swoon?" I ask her as I pick up the menu and finally settle in to select my dinner.

I never expect to hear a response, so when after a minute I hear a mumbled, "Maybe," coming from her direction I can't help but hide behind my menu with my growing smirk.

Dinner is delicious, as expected, as is the company. Kerry and Taylor regale us with some horror stories of terrible brides and events gone wrong. Right now Kerry is telling us about the time when the ring bearer got into the reception hall that was next to the church and ate his weight in cake before he was supposed to walk down the aisle. During his turn, he only made it halfway before he was vomiting all over the floor, and guests.

"So, not only did we have guests in their Sunday best now covered in projectile vomit, but we also had a ruined cake and a distraught bride," Kerry tacks on as Taylor adds, "But Kerry was a genius. Twenty minutes later she had the event moved outside and salvaged enough of the cake to pre-cut the slices while the bride and groom cut the top tier. It wasn't ideal, but given the circumstances, it couldn't have gone any better. The couple refers all of their engaged friends to us, which is how Elle heard of us. I think her son goes to school with the ring bearer."

"How long have you been doing this? I mean weddings?" I ask them, not knowing if they already mentioned it. Halfway through dinner and one of their stories, Sara placed her hand on my thigh mid-laugh and I lost all train of thought. All of my blood rushed straight to my cock and there is no hope of it returning any time soon.

"Professionally? About two years. But I've been hosting events ever since I can remember. It's like second nature to me," Kerry replies as she takes another sip of wine, the hint of an accent ringing in my ears. "Before we get started, tell me a little about both of you. How long have you been a couple?"

"Oh!" Sara exclaims at the same time I deny, "We're not. . ."

"I'm sorry, I shouldn't have assumed. You both just give off that vibe, that's all. I apologize for my mistake," Kerry rushes out her apology, and it's clear in her expression that she doesn't believe us one bit.

"That's okay. It's an easy mistake. Anyway, I'm Jackson's brother, obviously, and we co-own a landscaping company with our cousin. I'm also a detective."

Sara immediately jumps in. "I'm Elle's best friend, we've known each other since college. I'm her children's surrogate aunt. And I'm a divorce lawyer."

"Wow, it seems like you both live pretty demanding lives. What do you do for fun or during your downtime?"

Sara and I look over to each other and shrug. Neither of us really relax, it's something we've known about each other since we were introduced. Hell, I'm pretty sure I ended up leaving the cookout early for a call and Sara was on her phone with a client the entire time.

"We work," Sara states bluntly. "Look, I get that we're busy, but Elle and Jackson work more than we do, and I know that it's something they're working on for the future, but they asked for our help and we're going to adjust our schedules to help them. I actually have a meeting with my boss Friday to go over my workload, and I'm sure Cooper is doing the same."

I nod my head in agreement as Kerry jots a few notes in her tablet.

"Well, I'll take whatever time you have. Elle has requested the wedding in three months, and while that seems like a lot of time, it's really not. Luckily it will be early fall, so right after the busy season. Hopefully, we'll be able to secure a venue and caterer that is available. Because of the crunch, we need to get as much pinned down as soon as possible."

"We can make ourselves available," I reassure her as she flips her tablet around to show us a two-page checklist of items we need to make decisions on. I never knew it required more than picking a place and food.

"What I think would be the best decision moving forward is that we select one day each week to meet and make a decision. How do Saturdays work for each of you?"

I can sense the waves of irritation flowing off of Sara as she realizes that she's about to lose her one day of relaxation for the next few months.

"I'm available," I say as I reach for my glass of water and take a sip.

"Sara?" Kerry prompts and the jaw of my beautiful seatmate ticks in annoyance.

"I'll make it work. I just need to speak with my boss."

"Great. We'll I'll email you this list and make sure that Elle sends you her guest list. I need you to narrow that down as soon as possible. That gives us an idea of how many people we need to feed and lets us find a venue big enough. Let's get that done by Sunday, okay? In the meantime, let's plan on meeting the following Saturday to select the venues. It will be a full day."

"Okay, sounds good," I tell the women as they stand and retrieve their items preparing to leave the restaurant. Sara stays firmly seated on the bench, her teeth grinding against themselves. "Travel safe."

Once the women have moved from the table, I take a seat on the bench that they've vacated and bore my gaze into Sara.

"What's got you pissed off?" I question, and her eyes dart up at me. I suspect if it were possible smoke would fume from her ears.

"Every Saturday for three months? I thought it would be like maybe once a month, two at most." The stress of the situation radiates off of her and I hope that she is able to come up with some sort of solution.

"Maybe speak with your boss about the cases you have?"

"What? You mean tell them to stop sending me all of their work so that they can't play golf every afternoon? I'm sure that will go over well."

"What's the worst that could happen?"

"They fire me," she huffs.

"But we both know that isn't going to happen. Because then they'd have no one to pick up the slack."

She reaches out and begins to toy with the ends of the dessert menu the waitress left on the table, and without a second thought I reach out and place my hand on top of hers just as I had earlier, and she slowly brings her eyes up to meet mine.

"It will all work out, Sara. Order some dessert, I'll buy," I offer since Kerry and Taylor picked up our meal this evening.

"Why are you being so nice to me? Usually, most of our conversations are spent arguing."

Leaning forward I tug on her hand so that she leans across the table too; she's close enough that I can smell the sweetness of the white wine on her breath. It's intoxicating. "I'll tell you a secret," I begin, piquing her interest. "It's because I want to get in your pants." I shrug my shoulders casually taking in her shocked expression. She may be shocked, but her hand stays firmly entwined with mine, and she makes no motion to remove it.

"Why do I get the feeling that you're not joking?"

I shrug again and flag the waitress down when she passes by our table and I order us a large piece of chocolate cake. A buzzing sound surprises both of us and I instantly miss the loss of her touch as she reaches down for her phone.

"It's Elle," she tells me and then answers the call from her best friend, I'm assuming to check and see how the meeting has gone. They converse for a few minutes, and within that time the waitress brings out the decadent dessert, complete with her phone number written on a napkin facing my direction. I can't say that this isn't the first time a situation such as this has happened. It's not. It's even worse when Jackson and I go out in public together. We once had waitresses fighting over who would get to serve us. But now? Now I just feel sorry for the woman that she has to resort to these measures. I'm clearly here sitting with Sara, someone that has captured my eye since day one, even if she makes my blood boil most of the time.

"What's that?" she asks as she ends her call at the same time I'm balling up the napkin in my fist.

"Just someone being too presumptuous."

"You should hang on to it. You may need someone to fill your free time."

"But I only want one woman to fill up my free time," I imply as I take a forkful of cake and shove it in my mouth.

Smirking as a rosy blush grows on her cheeks, Sara leans onto her elbows and slices her fork through the dessert. "Oh really?"

"Yep. It's the same woman that told me to crawl up a chicken's ass when I hit on her."

"It's the only way you were going to get laid. And then I remember being told to get the stick out of my ass, promptly after which you called me Barbie."

"Ah yes. That's the woman."

"You're delusional, Cooper. If we hooked up someone is bound to think that the world is ending."

Placing one last hunk of cake on my fork, I wink in her direction. "Only because we'd be explosive, sweetheart."

"I'm not sure you can make that sort of assessment."

"Not an assessment. A promise. Come on, I'll walk you to your car."

Tossing a twenty dollar bill on the table to cover the dessert, I wait for Sara to hand me my jacket and then I press my hand to the middle of her lower back. Her body stiffens at first then relaxes into my touch. I wonder how her body would react as I stroke each inch of her skin. Something to consider another time as I try to control the firmness growing behind my pants envisioning Sara naked.

As we step outside a breeze whips around us and Sara's hair flows and twists around her face like a halo.

"Where did you park?" I ask as I steer us toward the parking lot, but she is reticent to follow.

"Actually, I walked. I'm not too far and it was a nice evening."

"You walked ten blocks?"

"Yes"

"In heels?" I add as I spare a glance down at her sexy but not sensible footwear. Not waiting for her response I tack on, "By yourself?"

She rolls those beautiful eyes and waves her hand in the air dismissing my comment.

"I've been taking care of myself for a long time, Cooper."

This independent streak she has is alluring as hell, but I know that we've had two females that were assaulted in this area just this month, so I wouldn't be able to forgive myself if something happened to Sara. She may hate it, but I'm standing my ground.

"Look, I'm giving you two options. One, you hop on the back of my bike and I drive you to your apartment or the second option is that I walk you the whole way. Either way, I'm accompanying you home."

"Seems a bit barbaric, even for you, Cooper."

"Just call me Tarzan. Make your choice, I need to get home and cuddle with Bailey."

"God forbid I keep you from your date."

Normally, I'd be thrilled to have a woman jealous over me, but I know Sara would claw my eyes out if ever given a chance.

Reaching out I slide my hand against her defiantly raised jaw.

"Bailey is the name of my dog, sweetheart."

"Oh," she says as she takes that plump bottom lip and sinks her teeth into the meaty flesh. "I think I remember Elle watching her a time or two. Cooper, I'm. . ." she begins, but I give her no chance of walking away from me.

"Come on, hop on the back of my bike. I'll give you the helmet and we'll have you home in just a few minutes."

Her body sits snuggly against my back and I am fighting everything I am not to run my hands up and down her thighs that cradle my hips. The drive is short, just a handful of minutes, until I'm pulling up in front of her complex. The short nails of her fingers dig into my stomach, but it's not an unwelcome sensation. I can imagine those fingers scratching down my back as I thrust myself deep inside her center.

Even as I kill the engine of the bike Sara's grip never waivers. I run my hands over her arms until our hands meet at the center of my abdomen.

"Sweetheart, we're here."

Like a bucket of ice has been poured over her, she pulls away from me and practically falls off the bike in her haste to gain space. I remove myself from the bike and then turn to help retrieve Sara from her perch. She stands, watching me through the helmet, her features barely visible through the tinted shield. I guide the protective wear from her head and while holding the helmet in one hand, I reach out and tuck a section of wayward hair behind her ear. Sara stares up at me with confusion swimming in her eyes. Confusion over herself or me, I'm not sure.

"Saturday, come by and we can start the guest list."

"I'll text you with a time." She chuckles and then grabs her phone from the bag she's placed across her body. "I don't even have your number."

I read out my digits and she shoots me a text so that I have hers as well.

"Okay, well, thank you for the ride, Cooper."

The woman doesn't give me a second to respond before she's turning on her heels and heading up the stairs to her place.

I know that people speak about phantom pains or the sensation of your phone vibrating even when it's not, but when I climb onto my bike, I can't help but still feel her arms wrapped tightly around me and damn if I don't wish that it were a reality.

74

Chapter Five

Sara

FOR TWO DAYS STRAIGHT all I've thought about is Cooper and it's driving me crazy. It was surreal having my hands on his muscled body – something that was far better than I ever could have imagined.

The clattering of ceramic placed on wood brings my attention back to my mother and her husband. Well, fifth husband. Since my father left us when I was five, my mother hasn't found anyone steady, hopping from one relationship to another. Their divorce was terrible, but instead of scarring my mother, she finds herself searching for love. Her newest husband, Oliver, has been around the longest. Unlike some of the others, I actually find his company tolerable. And he treats my mother like a queen.

"Hi, darling. You seem out of sorts today," my mother points out as she takes the seat next to me at their kitchen table. Oliver sets a plate of eggs and bacon in front of my mother and me before returning with his own.

"I'm fine. Just overwhelmed. I have a lot going on right now."

"A man, I hope?" my mother asks with a shimmer of hope in her eyes. Yes, mom, a man, but not in the way that you're hoping.

"No such luck, Mom."

"Well, tell me what's going on."

I take a few bites of the scrambled eggs and bacon before divulging my tale about my workload and how Elle has asked me to help get everything together for her wedding. I selfishly still believe that if she hired some help, she could make the time for herself. But then I immediately feel like a terrible friend.

"I have been getting handed the most difficult cases at work, which you know, typically I enjoy those kinds of challenges, but my colleagues are starting to take advantage of it, and I'm not even making a commission on them. And it's not fair that I spend extra hours at the office trying to catch up while they go play golf."

My mother nods her head in understanding while she hums against her coffee mug.

"I know I need to address it with them, and I plan to when I leave here. I scheduled a meeting with Mr.

Nemmer this morning, who, strangely enough, was available on a Saturday morning."

"But that's not all, is it?" she gently probes as she gazes over at her husband and then back to me.

"We met with the event planner Elle's hired on Thursday night and now I have to give up every Saturday for the next three months to help get everything squared away."

"We?"

"Er. . .yes. Jackson has asked his brother to help too because he's busy running the two businesses. I know that Elle and Jackson are working on both of them cutting back hours, but until that happens, they've asked us for help. I'm not even sure why they're getting married. For all I can tell they only see each other at night."

"They're getting married because they love each other, Sara. And I know that if Elle and Jackson say that they are working to spend more free hours together that they will. And you're a great friend to agree to help them."

"I think it's all a ruse to keep me from working so much."

"I can't say that I don't disagree. You're always working, sweetie. I worry about you. You're young and beautiful. This is when you should be having fun and finding your soul mate."

"Ha," I say exasperatedly. She knows how I feel about soul mates.

"Now, tell me about this brother. I can't help but notice how you blushed a bit as you mentioned him."

Apparently, I need to learn to control that reaction when I think about Cooper.

"He's uh. . .I mean, you met him at Elle's barbeque last year. Cooper. He co-owns one of the businesses with Jackson and their cousin, but he mainly works as a detective."

"Ah, yes. I do. Sweet boy. Handsome too."

"Whatever you say, Mom," I say around a forkful of food as I shovel the remainder into my mouth.

With a kiss on her cheek and a hug to Oliver, I leave my mother's house and head toward my office to have a few words with Mr. Nemmer.

I'm not surprised to find Mr. Nemmer's tiny convertible parked in the practice lot. What does surprise me is seeing the black SUV parked beside it. But then I suppose if he was going to be in the office he is probably seeing clients today.

Once inside I head directly to my office, not shocked to find a stack of files placed on my desk. Files of clients that Mr. Nemmer mentioned in our staff meeting yesterday as his new clients. Sifting through the pile my anger rises to a new degree when I count seventeen new cases. I barely have time for one right now.

With determination, I grab the files and stomp toward my boss's office not bothering to knock and hastily open his door. It takes me a moment to gather what's going on in front of me. Mr. Nemmer stands with his pants around his ankles while he awkwardly thrusts into a pinned Ms. Cullan as he presses her against his desk.

In a performance that I should win an award for, I keep a straight face and swallow down the urge to vomit. "Come see me in my office when you're done."

I head straight for the breakroom, not wanting to glance one more second at their stunned expressions, and grab a bottle of water from the staff fridge. I don't have to wait long before a red-faced Mr. Nemmer slithers into my office and stands in front of my desk with an authoritative gleam in his eye. Too bad I have zero desire to feed into his bullshit today.

"I don't want to know anything about what I saw. I'd rather not fill my head with those vile thoughts. But what I came to tell you today and why I called for a meeting is that I have zero interest in taking on the clients that you receive and yet you gain the commission for. I've been taken advantage of one too many times and I won't stand for it any longer."

Thrusting the stack of files into his chest, I'm mollified to see his weary expression, as if the man has forgotten how to practice law in all of these years.

"Also, I'm tired of working extra hours so that you and the boys can take the afternoons off. If you leave for the day, I'm going to leave for the day."

"So what are you saying, Ms. Campbell?"

"That I have the right to have your respect, and I expect it moving forward, or you can look forward to receiving my notice as I go find a practice that does appreciate me. I'm no longer spending my nights and weekends pouring over work at your hands. No more, Mr. Nemmer."

"Is that all?" he seethes as he begins to exit my office.

"Oh, and you can expect your little indiscretion to be noted in the Cullan divorce papers. I have my first meeting with them on Monday. I'm not sure how the husband is going to take to this can of worms you've opened up."

Without waiting for his response, I scoot passed him and exit my office. It's not until I'm in my car that I find my hands and body shaking from the adrenaline.

"Oh my God," I say to myself as I sit in my car with my hands perched on the steering wheel, my eyes glued to the building before me. Ms. Cullan's SUV has left and I watch as Mr. Neemer storms from the building carrying the files I so graciously bestowed upon him. I knew the man was sleazy from day one, but to have sex with a client? That's a new low.

This also means I get to spend a few hours updating my paperwork. Lovely.

A few hours later, I sit in my living room in the middle of a circle of papers. If anyone walked in right now, I'm afraid they'd think that they were interrupting some sort of ritual. I've made major headway on my cases as I note discrepancies and context changes throughout. The most time consuming was the addition to the Cullan case, adding in the witness of a separation period affair. The judge in our area doesn't take too kindly to post-marital relationships until a divorce is finalized.

I glance around the stack and with a heavy heart wonder when my life became a series of papers and notations. Growing up I always had such high aspirations and dreams. Things most little girls never dreamt of, but it was for me. I still wonder what my life would have been like if I had followed that path instead of the one I'm currently on.

Collecting the paperwork and putting them back into their respective files I head to my room with the hopes of taking a short nap to clear my head before going to Cooper's house, a place I have yet to step inside.

I'm surprised when I check my phone to see a couple of messages waiting for me.

Elle: List is done. Emailed it to you and Cooper. Brunch tomorrow?

Cooper: Got Elle's list.

I reply to Elle's message first and then Cooper's, letting him know that I'll be there in a few hours. I don't wait for a response from either party. Instead I tuck myself under the cool sheets of my bed and give my mind a chance to forget everything I saw this morning.

The music pulsates around us, the bass pounding out a rhythm that has the sea of bodies moving collectively as one. My vision is hazy, and I'm sure that someone has spiked my drink, but I don't care. All I want is to forget tonight. To forget my mother's recent divorce. To forget that my father hasn't contacted me in almost ten years. To forget that my boyfriend is screwing his professor. To forget life.

A pair of strong hands slides across my hips as they settle at the waistband of my denim skirt and with a gentle yank they pull me against a rock hard body. He doesn't fumble like many of the boys at our college. Even without turning around I can tell that he knows what he's doing.

For a few moments he sways his body with mine as we dance and the wretched stink of the frat house basement disappears and it's just this stranger and me moving as one. His hand travels under my shirt and across my rib cage, the sensation of his touch leaving me aching for more. Until he settles on the jagged scar on my hip.

I want to pull back, but the way he gently traces the line makes me believe that it's not an ugly part of me.

We continue to dance, my back to his chest, until I feel a vibration against my hip coming from his pants pocket.

"You have ten minutes to leave, sweetheart. This is the only warning I can give you."

I wake up gasping for air, the bits and pieces of the memory shocking my system. I want to remember more, yearn to see if this memory I had long since forgotten about but one that sticks with me subconsciously, will ever offer a glimpse of my savior's face. It never does.

I remember finding my roommate and leaving the frat house, but I woke that next morning in Elle's room. There was talk that the party had been broken up, which was a typical occurrence, and a lot of the members were arrested for underage drinking and drugs by the campus police. And the news spoke about investigations in a prostitution ring.

Those hands though. It was the first time in my life that I had felt something new, something unfamiliar. Comfort. And from a complete stranger nonetheless. I never even saw the stranger's face.

But as I tug on a pair of jeans, I smile at the memory of the stranger's hands. It's the first time I've remembered that part of that night and the butterflies in my stomach flutter wildly at the thought.

Needing a distraction, I grab a random T-shirt from my dresser, slip it over my body and then grab a bottle of water as I head out the door. As I settle in the car I take a moment to let the Bluetooth connect to my phone, then I dial Cooper's number to ask if he has eaten and if he wants me to grab anything. But, as it seems to be a common occurrence recently, he surprises me by saying that he plans on cooking. I wasn't aware that he, or most men, knew how to cook more than bacon, eggs, and steak. Of course, I shouldn't get my hopes up since he'll probably end up serving steak and potatoes.

During the drive over to Cooper's house, I try to distract my thoughts by singing along to the radio, but nothing works. Flashes from memory keep pushing through, leaving me more confused than before.

I pull into Cooper's driveway, noting that Jackson, Elle, and the kids don't seem to be home. The walk down the path to the house's front door feels like I'm walking toward my own execution. My palms are sweaty and I feel a bit disoriented. After the events with Mr. Nemmer this morning and the dream this afternoon I'm not in the right frame of mind to bicker with Cooper tonight. Hopefully, he'll go easy on me and we won't argue over the guest list.

"Hey," he says as he opens the door before I have a chance to knock. My mouth hangs open in awe as I take him in. He wears a pair of well-worn black jeans that have holes tattered into certain areas. I catch a glimpse of his muscled thigh through one of the tears and I find myself wishing that I could lick that teasing patch of skin. The black T-shirt threatening to rip in two against the muscles while his biceps stretch the short sleeves to their maximum, highlights Cooper's taut chest. His hair is damp as if he just took a shower. It lazily flops over his head drawing my attention to his blue eyes. The blue eyes taking in every inch of my body as well.

"Hi." I stand before him and lick my suddenly dry lips. For the first time in a year, I'm actually nervous to be alone in a room with Cooper, like a virginal teenager anticipating her first kiss.

He takes my hand and tugs me inside, dragging me straight through his house toward the kitchen. I barely have a chance to shut the door behind me.

"Have a seat, dinner will be ready in a minute," he tells me as a dog rushes over with her tail wagging wildly and places her head on my lap. "That's Bailey."

"Oh, well, hello, Bailey. I've heard very little about you, but I know that you like cuddles and my niece and nephew." Elle had laughed herself into hysterics when I mentioned to her over the phone about my embarrassing conversation with Cooper and the mention of Bailey.

The dog practically purrs as I stroke her head and Cooper turns around and laughs at the sight of us before he turns back to the stove and pulls a dish from the oven.

"So, want to tell me what's up?" Cooper suggests as he places the dish on a potholder in the middle of the table. The aroma from the baked lasagna fills the space with a delicious tomato and cheese scent.

"What do you mean?"

"When you pulled up you had this look on your face – a bit frightened, a bit confused, and a bit angry. It's not a combination I see a lot."

"It's nothing you need to worry about. This smells delicious by the way."

He cuts up the pasta and divvies it onto our plates, smiling as he hands me my portion. We sit together silently, but when I take my first hearty bite of the pasta, I lean back in my chair, close my eyes, and groan so deeply that my entire body vibrates in delight.

"This is the best lasagna I have ever tasted, Cooper."

"Thanks. I'll be sure to tell my mom. It's her recipe."

Taking another bite, I don't even bother to look up from my plate as I scoop the food into my mouth. "Did your mother teach you how to cook as well?"

"She did," he says as he chuckles, before handing me a napkin.

"Oh gosh, I must be a mess. I'm eating like a toddler." Embarrassed, I hastily wipe the food from my face; the blush I know is evident on my cheeks growing when I look at the large red splotches on the cloth that must have been all over my face.

"No, you're beautiful," he counters. It's not the first time I've been called beautiful, but it is the first time someone sounds like they genuinely mean it. "So, are you going to tell me now what had you out of sorts when you got here?" Cooper asks again as he pushes his empty plate to the side and leans his elbows on the table. The veins in his forearms ripple and twist as he positions them under his chin. I've always loved a good pair of muscled arms and Cooper's are by far some of the sexiest I've ever seen.

"Is this why you fed me first?"

"Maybe."

"Do I get dessert if I answer?"

"Probably."

"What are we having?"

"Let's leave a few surprises between us, sweetheart. Stop stalling."

"Fine. Well, it started with a visit to my Mom's this morning, who recently got married again for the fifth or sixth time. She was giving me crap about still being single."

He grins and shakes his head. "Of course she was, she's your mother. She wants to make sure that there is someone to take care of you."

"I can take care of myself."

"We all know that, sweetheart, but sometimes it's nice to let someone else hold the reigns for a while. I know that that isn't all, tell me more."

I sigh and then dive into what I witnessed at my office this morning and how it throws a huge wrench in the already difficult case I'm working on.

"Is that everything?" he probes and I tug at my bottom lip as I consider telling him about the memory that I'm not so sure isn't just a dream.

I take a deep breath and close my eyes before I lean forward and wrap my arms around my body. "I took a nap earlier because I haven't been sleeping well and I'm exhausted. But I started having this dream that seemed more like bits and pieces of a memory I've stashed away in my mind. It doesn't make sense, and when I try to bring it forward, I get nothing but blanks.

"Memory repression. It's usually due to trauma or stress. Do you remember anything happening?"

"No, that's the thing. At the end of the memory clips, I'm at Elle's dorm. It's so confusing, and I'm trying to piece it together, but I keep coming up short."

Wordlessly he stands from the chair, the legs scratching against the tiled floor, and reaches into the fridge to retrieve what I'm assuming is dessert. I'm pleasantly surprised when he sets a small dessert plate holding a slice of cherry cheesecake.

"Is this the boxed Jell-O cheesecake?" I ask in awe.

Running his hand along his scruff covered jawline, he nods in reply.

"How did you know that this is my favorite?"

"A nosy neighbor may have put the bug in my ear."

"Well, I'll be sure to thank her for that. She's a fantastic baker, and I love everything she makes, but something about this is just. . .yummy."

I'm so lost in the flavors of the cake that I only just hear a growl from across the room and at first I think it's Bailey, but as I slowly pull the fork from my mouth, wanting to savor every last morsel, I notice a look in Cooper's eyes. Something fierce and territorial. He stands abruptly from the table and grabs my plate, his free hand clenching in a fist and then releasing just as quickly.

As he stands hunched over his sink scrubbing the dishes as if they've personally insulted him, I can't help but wonder what I've done to cause this reaction in him. Or that maybe I was the one that insulted him somehow.

Moving from the table, I go to stand beside him at the counter and gently rest my hand on his shoulder. "Cooper, I. . ."

"Don't," he rumbles as he finishes drying the last of the plates.

While still leaning over the sink, his hands clasping the edge of the counter, he tilts his head to look over at me. The tension between us is thick and heavy, as if a dense fog has settled around us. I'm not sure if he's going to slant his body and kiss me or argue with me over something.

Licking my lips, I notice that his eyes go directly to my mouth and I'm afraid of what I'll do if he does kiss me. Then I'm left wondering what it would feel like to have his lips pressed against mine, to feel his body responding to me.

"I'm. . ugh. . .going to go get started on the guest list," I whisper and reluctantly turn around and leave the kitchen before I throw myself at him. Which is the most frustrating part because I don't need a distraction like him in my life.

On my way out of the room, I snag my bag from the back of the kitchen chair where I had placed it when I arrived and I move into the living space assuming the layout is the same as Elle's, and luckily it is.

I'm surprised to find the place warm and inviting, not like the bachelor pad I had expected. The walls are a very light brown, almost a cream color, and the trim has all been repainted white. I settle against the leather fabric of his couch, shocked that it's not cold and stiff, but soft and supple as it conforms to my body. A few decorative items hold a place of purpose on the built-in bookshelves and on the coffee table before me. Truthfully, the room has a very feminine touch, the only masculine thing I notice is the overly large television mounted above the fireplace.

"I'm sorry."

Startled, I jump in my seat with a gasp when Cooper takes his seat beside me, very close beside me.

He continues, "I was being rude in the kitchen, it wasn't anything you did."

"Okay."

We sit in silence, the awkwardness blooming at an alarming rate to the point where I force myself to make conversation.

"So, I like this room. Did you do it yourself?"

I watch as he turns his penetrating gaze away from me and looks around the room as if seeing it for the first time.

"My. . .uh. . .mom helped. I didn't want any of Jackson's furniture, so we gave it all to charity."

"I've only spoken to her a couple of times, but she seems like a great woman. Especially since she handles you and your brother so well," I add in jest, and it finally seems to break through the steel wall Cooper threw up after dinner. "Anyway, let's get started on this. I'm not sure how long this may take, but with Elle and Jackson's budget we can only allow fifty people."

"Yikes, that would be just my family."

"Well, we're in luck because Elle and her family are working on things, but since her divorce, they still aren't on the best of terms." When he looks at me with confusion, I elaborate. "They sided with her ex during the divorce. At least at the beginning, even though he cheated and knocked up one of her close friends."

"What a douche."

"I know, and she's had a hard time forgiving her parents for that betrayal. But they're working on it. So I can't imagine that she'd have a lot of outside relatives attending."

"Okay, let me print a copy and we can take a look."

I feel a sense of loss as he stands from the couch and moves down the hall, but I'm not left alone for long. He returns with a sullen look in his eyes and I'm beginning to dread the words about to come from his mouth.

"It looks like we're in for a long night." He grimaces as he fans out twenty pieces of paper across the coffee table. Ten full sheets of names and addresses.

We get to work narrowing down the selections. I tackle Elle's side and Cooper tackles his brother's. Just when I think I've got a handle on my list, I can feel the darkness closing in and my lids begin to close on their own. And without a second thought, I allow my body to slouch against the muscled shoulder beside me as I welcome the sleep.

Chapter Six

Cooper

THE LIGHTEST OF TOUCHES feather across my chest as I inhale the sweet scent of honey and vanilla, two of my favorite flavors. I smile in my sleep and try to adjust my shoulder. That's when I realize that my head is resting on my arm draped across the seat cushion of the couch and I have my other arm wrapped tightly around a woman. Particularly a sleeping woman that is snuggling against my chest.

I try not to move us too much, but as I try to resettle myself, she alters her body as well. I fear that she'll move away or panic, but to my surprise, she adjusts her leg between mine and somehow manages to bring her body closer to mine. The arm I have wrapped around her waist tightens out of reflex and I drift back to the most peaceful sleep that I've had in weeks.

It's been a week since I became a downright bastard. My piss poor mood has my colleagues and the recruits running in the other direction when I enter a room. Even Jackson called me out on my disposition during our weekly meeting on Wednesday. He says I'm throwing a temper tantrum worse than Noah's. I've seen that kid throw a fit, so Jackson must be exaggerating.

Today as I sit at the kitchen table at their house waiting on Elle to get back from her first catering drop off of the day, hopefully with a few of her scones to spare, Jackson badgers me to tell him why I've developed such a bad temper.

I don't want to tell the truth, and I am not even sure I can say it without feeling the ache in my chest, the same one that I felt last Sunday when I woke up to find Sara gone. No goodbye, no note, just a room filled with regret. It's not as if I intentionally kept her there when she fell asleep, but I knew it was safer for her to sleep than to drive while tired. Of course, when her head fell onto my shoulder, I couldn't help myself and I draped my arm over her shoulder, simply to make her more comfortable. I kept working and then the next thing I knew I was asleep with her on the couch.

The worst part is that she won't even speak to me. Not in call or text. I've even been trying to catch her at her place, but I didn't want to come off as a stalker. Which now that I think about it may not have been a bad idea.

"So? Are you going to tell me why your temper has gone up ten notches?" my brother says with a jab to my arm effectively bringing me back to the moment.

"I'd rather not tell you."

"You don't have a choice, because if you don't tell me, Elle is going to be pissed at me. And if she is pissed at me, I'm going to be an ass – to you in particular. So just cut the crap and tell me."

"I slept with Sara," I blurt out without thinking. "Wait, no-" I try to explain but my brother's hand swats against my head.

"You couldn't keep it in your pants for three months, Coop?"

"It's not like that! We did sleep together, but we didn't. . .you know. . ." I gesture with my head to the living room where the two kids are watching a movie. "She fell asleep at my house last weekend while we were working on your guest list. Then the next morning she was just – gone. She must have freaked out or something. I don't know, but it pisses me off." I cradle my head in my hands hating how raw I feel talking about my feelings, especially the ones involving a woman.

A burst of laughter explodes in the kitchen and I look up from my palms to find Jackson bent over, his shoulders bouncing with each laugh.

"Oh, man," he says between hoots, wiping fake tears from his eyes for good measure. "You should hear yourself right now."

"This is why I don't talk to you. And now you've pissed me off even further. Great job."

The chair almost tilts over in my haste to leave the table.

"Hey, man," he begins. "I didn't mean anything by it. I've never seen you torn up over a woman before, it's usually the other way around. And Sara of all people. I didn't even think it was wise to put you two in a room together with the way you pick fights with each other."

"You're not making it better."

"Look, maybe she was scared. She doesn't do relationships and for her to feel comfortable falling asleep at your house says a lot. That was a big step and maybe she needed time to think about it."

"Then why doesn't she answer my calls or texts?"

"Think about Sara for a moment. She's incredibly independent and self-sufficient. She's never needed anyone's help. I know for a fact that she hasn't been sleeping well, so much so that we were afraid to have her watch the kids for a while because she just looked so damn exhausted. So you gave her something that she desperately needed and didn't even ask for."

"Sleep?"

"Sleep, a friend, a sense of not feeling lonely. Oh, look, Mom is here to watch the kids. I've got to head to the gym to finish training this manager so I can free up some time. Good luck with the Sara situation. And for what it's worth I think you two would work out."

"I'm not even sure that I like her."

"Don't kid a kidder. You'd be an idiot not to like her. And you, brother, are not an idiot. Enjoy venue hunting. Don't be an ass and pick a shitty place."

"Yeah, like Sara would let me do that."

He leaves the room with a chuckle and greets our mother as I slip out the back door and walk across the yard back to my place. If Jackson noticed my change in demeanor, I know that my mother would interrogate me ten times more. I learned my skills from her, after all.

The trio of women ooh and aah over the details of the museum's ballroom. Hell, I didn't even know that you could have a party at a museum, let alone a wedding reception! But my attention isn't on the details or the coordinator's suggestions of where to put the tables, my focus is completely on the woman that has ignored my gaze since we arrived.

She stepped out of her car and walked right past me with her head down, ignoring my non-verbal pleas to speak with me.

"Mr. Divers, what do you think about having the dance floor off to the side, or would you prefer it to be in the middle?"

"Middle," I reply bluntly as I lean toward the woman currently staring at the ceiling as if it holds the answers to every question ever asked. "I need to talk to you and I'm not taking no for an answer."

Straggling behind the women as they walk across the space my eyes follow the sway of one particular lady's hips as she takes each step.

"So, what do you all think?" Kerry asks and I shrug my shoulders.

"No."

"What?" Sara questions as she finally looks my way.

"Jackson would hate it. Afraid he'd break something."

Dawning shows on her face. "Oh, yeah, you're right. Sorry. Let's go to the next one."

We collectively walk out of the museum and before she can move toward her car, I grab Sara's arm and steer her toward my car.

"What are you doing?"

"We'll come back to get your car, but we need to talk, Sara." I practically shove her into the passenger seat, not giving her a chance to escape.

"Why did you sneak out?" I ask her once I'm settled into the car and begin the trek to the next location. She never responds until we reach the bed and breakfast on the outskirts of the city.

"I freaked out. I'm sorry, but I woke up from like the single best night of sleep I've ever had and I was wrapped all around you and I freaked. I got out of there as fast as I could and I haven't slept since. And you know what? I am so tired." The sound of her voice breaking at the end of her statement breaks my heart.

I know that Jackson had thought that maybe she had been scared, but it didn't sink in until this very moment.

"Sara. . ." I begin, but a knock sounds on her window as Taylor and Kerry arrive with bright grins on their faces. I watch her exit the car more determined than ever to get her alone and talk things over.

An older couple and their coordinator greet us at the entrance and we follow them through the courtyard where the ceremony would be held and the small pavilion where a reception could take place. It's quaint and would definitely suit Elle, but I could see Jackson being miserable. Especially since he has requested that I search out a bed and breakfast for them to stay at for their honeymoon.

The couple takes us inside and shows us the area where the men could get ready and then takes us to the bridal suite. The women look around the space as if it actually matters where Elle is going to get ready. Sara steps past me and leans across the doorjamb to check out the bathroom, and when she's close enough, I twist her around and pin her against my body and the wall out of the view of everyone else.

"Why are you running from me?"

"I don't do this, Cooper. Whatever this is."

"It was just two people that fell asleep on the couch, Sara. It doesn't have to be anything more than that."

"You're sure? How come you're not freaking out?"

"I'm more angry that you left without a trace, I almost thought that I dreamt the entire thing."

"Oh."

"When all I really wanted to do was kiss you."

"You want to kiss me?" she asks in shock, as if the thought never crossed her mind.

"Right now? More than my next breath," I reveal to her as I lean closer, and brush my lips against hers with a feather's touch.

Something happened in the year we've spent arguing and bickering that turned her from his frustratingly beautiful woman to this alluring morsel that I just needed to have a taste of. And as I brush my lips across hers again, I find that I could quickly become addicted to her.

"I. . .I don't think that's such a good idea."

Against her mouth, I reply, "I never said that it was." I pull back so that we're only a breath apart, enough space that only a thin slip of paper could slide between us, and I wait. I wait to see her run, I wait to see if she pushes me away, I wait to see if she pulls me closer. But she doesn't do any of those things. She licks those beautiful lips and then whispers, "I'm not ready for you. I'm not sure I'll ever be ready."

"Sara, look at me," I demand as I lift her face toward mine and slide my hand in her hair, her head tilting into my palm as a reflex. "I want you. I don't know when it happened, maybe it was all of the arguing, maybe it was that night on my couch, or maybe it was something more because I've felt a connection with you since the beginning that I've tried to ignore but I can't any longer. And I think that you want me too. I'll be patient with you, sweetheart. I'm in no rush. But for what it's worth, I think you are ready because deep inside you know that no matter what, I would never hurt you."

"What are you asking me?" she whispers.

Unable to control myself I lean forward and run my nose up her exposed neckline, from her shoulder to her ear, savoring the hitch of her breath at my touch. "It can be a relationship, or it can be just sex. I'll take whatever you can give me."

"What if I can't do either?"

"Then I'll just have to work harder to convince you that you can. Don't make the decision now, think about it." Boldly I reach out and grab her hand placing it directly over the stiffness in my pants. "Think long and hard about it."

She gasps and then, as I expected, she rolls her eyes and pulls her hand away. "You're so barbaric."

"I'll do whatever I have to. Come on, they're probably looking for us."

Grabbing her hand and holding it tight enough so that she can't pull it away I take us down the steps from the bridal suite and meet the group out on the front porch. Now, instead of ignoring me, Sara refuses to make eye contact with the rest of the group.

"So," Kerry begins, "what do you all think?"

"I think the space is nice and I know Elle and Jackson would appreciate the option of getting ready in the rooms on the property. It's definitely one to keep on the list, " Sara speaks up.

Kerry's smile beams as she scurries off and relays our thoughts to the owners, leaving us standing with Taylor as she looks around the place.

"Taylor, where did you grow up?" I ask, trying to start a conversation with the woman we haven't spent a lot of time with.

"Uh, here and there," she replies vaguely.

Dashing through the front doors, Kerry glances down at her watch and then back up to us. "We have a few more places to look at and we're running a little behind schedule," she adds as a jab toward me. I'm sure for keeping Sara occupied for a few extra minutes.

"Well, then let's go."

The remainder of the morning and the afternoon are spent traipsing around the city. We stop at two more bed and breakfasts, three hotels, and a botanical garden. By the time we get in the car to head to the last location, I'm exhausted and starving.

"Is this over yet?"

With a groan, Sara replies, "Just one more."

I spare a glance in her direction as we sit at the stoplight, entranced at the way the sun illuminates her hair and profile. Her lips are parted slightly and her eyelids are closed. And if I didn't know any better, I'd think that she was asleep.

Except her saucy mouth interrupts the silence again. "Stop staring at me."

"Can't help it."

"Well, try."

"Why would I want to stop staring at an angel?"

"Because it will blind you." Opening her eyes, she looks over at me with a curious expression. "Are you just trying to get in my pants or do you really mean that?"

"What? That you look like an angel? I mean it, I don't lie. And if I were trying to get into your pants, then I'd come out with guns blazing. But I'm trying to take it slow."

"Well, I appreciate that. Oh, I think that's it over there." She points to the old train station.

"Huh, this is kind of cool," I tell her as we exit the car, Sara stepping from the vehicle before I have the chance to assist.

"I didn't even know you could do anything with the space. I guess let's see what the inside looks like."

We follow Kerry and Taylor into the space and I'm immediately taken aback by the structure. It's been beautifully restored.

"Alright, here is the last spot for the day. This is the old Third Street Station built in 1901 and restored in 2005. The space actually has two venues we can choose from, one being this area which was restored to its Victorian grandeur. It can seat 800 or 500 with a dance floor and it has a bridal suite available.

"The second venue is on the second floor, overlooking the city. It's been given a very modern touch with exposed beams and bricks and floor to ceiling windows that look over the city. It's a smaller space that can accommodate 300 or 150 with a dance floor. Would you like for me to show you around?"

"Yes, please." Sara claps enthusiastically.

I know without even having a look that the modern space is going to be the winner. It's very much so what Jackson and Elle are looking for. She can even add her rustic touches to the space.

An arm slides through mine and I'm surprised as Sara links us together as we walk around the first venue. It's massive and grand and a space I could envision Kerry in, even in the short time that I've known her.

Kerry guides us up a massive flight of stairs to the upstairs and I don't even have to look around the space to know that this is it. This is the space we've been on our never-ending quest for today.

And with the way Sara catches her breath and grips my arm I know that she knows it too.

"Wow," she murmurs and I nod at her sentiment.

"So, what do you all think about this space?" Taylor gestures with her arm as if she were on a game show.

"This is perfect," Sara tells them and then asks how Kerry plans to lay out the ceremony and dinner.

Together they watch as Kerry draws the layout on her tablet and explains how the transitions will happen between the space to separate the ceremony and reception. She discusses the dance floor and our catering options, which luckily Elle and Jackson have already discussed with the planner.

"Well, I think that we've made excellent progress today. Next week we're scheduled for linen choice and cake tasting. I received the guest list and have sent them off to the calligrapher to begin addressing the envelopes. Elle has already selected the invitations and thank you cards."

Taylor pipes in as she glances up from her tablet. "Do we know if there is a vision for the reception? Any pictures or themes that Elle and Jackson have suggested?"

"Oh, I have an entire notebook." Sara looks up at me and I shoot her a grin.

"Well, for homework you two go through the ideas you've been presented and please have an idea for me by Wednesday. I need to see what items we can purchase or rent."

"We can get started on it tonight," I say, as I hastily grab Sara's hand and tug her behind me as I swiftly exit the building.

"Oh, I have a text from Elle. She and Jackson want to know if we can meet them for dinner across town. The company that will be catering the reception ordered some of her pies and opened up a table for them."

"Damn," I murmur under my breath as we approach the car. I had been hoping to have the chance to spend more time alone with Sara, but it seems like my brother and his fiancée have other plans in mind.

"Is that okay?" She peers up at me innocently and I know that I can't deny her anything. "Sure, it's fine. Did you want me to bring you back to your car now?"

"Yeah, that's probably best," she says almost sullenly.

Don't worry, sweetheart, I feel the same way.

Chapter Seven

Sara

W ATCHING COOPER STRUT IN front of the car as he moves to the driver's side is so hypnotic and sexual that I jump in my seat when he slams the door closed. I'm lost in my own Cooper-filled world and I'm not sure I want to break free. Since we left the first bed and breakfast this morning, all I can focus on is how soft Cooper's lips felt against mine. There was a spark of awareness that traveled from my lips down to my toes and it was so apparent that I couldn't deny it even if I tried.

My hesitation in his request isn't because I'm not attracted to him – I would have to be blind not to be, and even then just the feel and smell of him would garner me in lust. I'm not even sure if it's that I'm so jaded by broken relationships that I steer clear of them at all costs, though I'd be a fool to deny that it is quite the possibility. I think my fear stems from the fact that Cooper makes me feel something that I never have before – alive, whole. Just those sensations today are things that I'm afraid to give up with how powerful they make me feel. But one thing I know is that by being whole, Cooper could be the one to break me. You can't destroy something that isn't there, but I'm not sure I can survive Cooper. But oh how I long to.

I'm so lost in my thoughts that I don't realize when we've pulled up at the museum where my car sits in the empty parking lot. Cooper exits and walks around the hood of the car to let me out, something I'm learning he's adamant about if his seething gaze when my hand reached for the door handle is any indication.

I wish that I had the nerve to ask him to come back to my place after dinner, just to talk or watch reality television. Something about being in Cooper's presence recently puts me at ease, which is the opposite of how the two of us used to interact.

"I'll follow you there," Cooper tells me as I press the key fob to unlock the vehicle and he opens the door for me.

"Okay."

We arrive at the restaurant and I search out Elle and Jackson, gripping my purse in my hands so that I don't reach out and grab Cooper instead. Elle spots us from the corner and we walk through the crowded restaurant toward the large table where Elle and Jackson sit with their two little angels beside them coloring on sheets of paper.

"Hey, guys." I wave at the group as I grip the back of the seat to pull it away from the table, but Cooper beats me to it. Once I sit down, he gently pushes the chair back under the table, his finger trailing against the skin exposed along my shoulders from my boatneck shirt. My body shivers at the contact.

As he settles himself in his chair, he makes sure that we're sitting as close to each other as possible, which leaves a gaping space at the table. Elle and Jackson look at the space and then back over to us and then repeat the motion. Of course, Cooper takes that moment to lean his arm against the back of my chair. If I could bury myself and hide in this very moment, I would.

"So. . ." Elle prompts and I just shake my head and grab her glass of wine from across the table and chug it thoroughly.

"Did you get all your things delivered today, Elle?" Cooper asks and I silently pray to the heavens that he's able to steer the conversation.

"I did, thanks."

"Darn, I was hoping you'd have some goodies left over for me to take home."

"Cooper, you know I can always have snacks ready for you. Just ask."

"Naw, you're busy enough. So, bro, how is the training going?"

Thrilled with Cooper's distraction I lean over to Kennedy and ask to see what she's coloring on her paper – a unicorn.

"Hey, I was thinking I could watch the kids one weekend for you if you and Jackson wanted to get away. I know that you need to plan it out with your business and things, but maybe just a night away could be good." I don't glance up as I offer my babysitting services to Elle because she knows I mean it. Since I'm doubtful that I'll have children of my own one day, I enjoy spending as much time with her kids as I can.

"I do have a weekend that we could get away, if you don't mind. You'd need to pick up Noah from school."

"That's no problem, just let me know the day and time."

"I bet Cooper would help too," Elle throws out as she takes a sip of her water and flags down the waiter. "Want to tell me what's going on with that?"

"If I knew, I'd tell you. I'm not really sure, to be honest. But. . ." I say as I look over my shoulder at him and he smiles in return before continuing his conversation with Jackson. "But I may be willing to take a chance. Geez, I'm giving myself whiplash. I'm turning into one of those wishy-washy females that I can't stand."

"If it's any consolation, I'm proud of you."

"Don't be, this could all very well blow up in my face. I'm not even sure why I'm taking the risk. There is just something about him. All that arguing? Maybe it was me fighting the attraction," I whisper to her. "And when he almost kissed me, Elle, it took all my strength not to sink into him."

"Whoa, he kissed you?" she whisper-shouts, her eyes the size of the bread dishes on the table.

"Almost. It was like a brush in passing and I wanted so much more."

"What are you ladies talking about that has Elle turning into a tomato?"

We both turn our heads so quickly in the direction of the men at the table that we most likely have whiplash.

"We're not talking about anything important. Just her bachelorette party," I quip, hoping to nip this conversation in the bud.

The waiter stops by the table just as Jackson shouts, "No!" and I'm almost afraid the poor man is going to scurry away never to return. But luckily Cooper asks him to bring a round of waters.

"She's getting a party. Just like I'm sure Cooper will take you to some strip club."

"No, Elle doesn't want that," Jackson snarls as his fiancée glares at him. "Maybe I do."

I watch as the two start to argue and I turn to look at Cooper, and I shrug my shoulders.

"Is this what we look like when we argue?"

Something glimmers in his eyes as he watches his brother speak to Elle in a forceful, but kind tone as he tries to reason with her.

Cooper turns back to me and replies, "No, because at least they'll get makeup sex out of this. Maybe next time?"

I can't help but laugh which in turn brings our companions' attention back to me.

"We're just staying at the house with a few friends, Jackson. Chill out."

"Fine," he says, but then he makes it a point to look deeply at Cooper. "But no strip clubs."

It's our weekly staff meeting and everyone looks just as thrilled to be sitting at the conference table as I am. The only person I'm pleased to see is Janice the secretary because she is the only one in the room that is genuinely a nice person, everyone else would rather spit on you than help you.

Mr. Nemmer stands at the front of the room going over our current client listing and court dates.

"Ms. Campbell, can you give us an update on the Cullan case? It's beginning to get a lot of local press and interest."

"The only update I have for you is that the other lawyer and I are doing our best to keep this out of the courts. It had been an uncontested divorce until recent information has been brought to light," I mention. I don't throw out there that it's the affair Ms. Cullan is currently having with Mr. Nemmer, but I do bring up the one the husband's private investigator has brought to light. "Ms. Cullan has also optioned to hire a private investigator because she is certain that one of their executives had a child by him. Honestly, it's turning into a big mess and I do not appreciate it being handed to me along with everyone else's scraps so that you have it easy." The outburst surprises me and I can tell by the look on the other lawyers' faces that it surprises them too. Anger has been steadily building inside of me since I took this new position and it finally boiled over.

Nerves seem to get the better of my boss as his face pales, he knows that I haven't mentioned his indiscretion to the team but I haven't had a chance. I'm not blackmailing him, all I want is to be treated like everyone else. "Yes, er. . .Ms. Campbell, I believe we discussed some resolutions to the matter."

"Let's make sure that we adhere to it." Because every day that passes, I consider leaving them all in the lurch and quitting. I have enough money saved that I could take some time to find a new position.

After the meeting, Janice follows me to my office and asks about Elle and the wedding planning. She's met Elle a handful of times when my friend stopped by to bring me lunch or treats. I haven't told her what I witnessed on that Saturday a few weekends ago, but I wouldn't be surprised if she already knows. She is the eyes and ears of this practice.

She settles into the chair across from my desk and I ask her how her paralegal classes are going, something she's been working toward for a few years. She is in her final semester of classes now.

"Are you going to tell me what happened back in the meeting?"

"Which part? The one where I finally stood up for myself or the part where my case is getting out of control?"

"Both?"

"Well, the Cullans are just out to get each other, it's turning vindictive. And I really don't want to be tied into that."

"I knew that case would be trouble from day one. Now, what about when you stood up for yourself?"

"Yes, it was a long time coming. I thought it was just part of settling into a new routine, but work began to take over my life and it was becoming too much. Do you know that last weekend was the first time since I can remember that I didn't bring work home?"

"I, for one, am glad to see you put your foot down. They were taking advantage of you and I'm happy to see that you called them out on it."

A text pings on my phone and a picture of Cooper pops up behind the message. Before I can reach for it Janice's eyes light up at the sight of him.

"Please tell me that he is the reason you want more free time?"

"Uh, part of the reason. He is Elle's soon to be brother-in-law."

"In the few years you've worked here I've never seen you with anyone. I was beginning to wonder if you swung for the other team. Regardless, I'm excited for you. I hope it all works out."

"Me too, we're supposed to meet up tonight."

Janice stands and walks backward to the doorway of my office. "Well, then I suggest you get to work because I am kicking you out of the building at five sharp."

I chuckle at her retreat and then get to work so that I can leave on time.

The remainder of my day runs smoothly and, as promised, at 5 p.m. Janice knocks on my door and tells me to get out. Cooper and I arranged to meet at my apartment to go over the themes and ideas Elle and Jackson have put in the notebook when he gets off from work at six. It is easier for him since his office isn't far from my apartment.

The first thing I do when I walk through the door of my place is pick up the empty carton of ice cream that sits precariously on the edge of my coffee table. I spent some time going over my conversation with Cooper from this weekend and I needed some help from my friends Ben and Jerry.

In the kitchen, I begin to make a taco casserole for dinner. I check the clock once I place the dish in the oven and see that I have enough time to hop in the shower before Cooper should be arriving.

I don't linger in the shower. Instead I run in, wash off, and get out. For a moment I consider putting on something sexy and alluring, but I hang my head with a shake. Who am I kidding? Cooper has already seen me in my loungewear and business suits. Instead, I opt to throw on a pair of jean shorts and a tank top.

The casserole still has about twenty minutes left before it's done, so I settle back on the couch and turn on the television, but I don't see any of the images flashing on the screen. I stare at the wall wondering what I'm doing with Cooper. Someone that used to grate on my every nerve now has them pulsating at the thought of his touch. I've never craved someone the way that I suddenly want him.

The oven timer sounds and I jump from my seat, startled that so much time has passed. I let the casserole cool on the counter as I return to the couch. Cooper had texted that he would be at my place around six so when the clock shows the time as seven I begin to worry.

Another fifteen minutes pass and I decide to plate my dinner, but just as I cut into the casserole a knock on the door resonates in the room, and my heart begins to pound. I put down the spatula and make my way to the door just as another knock follows. The flutters in my stomach intensify as I place my hand on the doorknob.

Am I ready for this? Ready for whatever may or may not happen?

Opening the door, I'm caught off guard as Cooper rushes toward me. His hands slide against my face and delve into my hair as he slams his lips against mine.

"Tell me that you don't want this," he whispers as he kisses me once more.

Letting my heart speak for me I tell him, "I do. I want you, I want this."

"Thank fucking God," he murmurs as he moves his hands to wrap around the back of my thighs and lifts me in the air against him, my legs wrap around his waist reflexively. "I'm sorry I'm late, I got caught up on a case and lost track of time."

I return his kiss then say, "I won't hold it against you this time."

He turns and presses me against the wall with a clang, the picture frames shaking with the motion. My back arches as I groan against his mouth, my lips parting in welcome of his demanding tongue. He's tentative at first, wanting to make sure that he isn't pressing me for more than I'm ready for. I accept his intrusion willingly.

Cooper pulls back from me, his eyes staring into mine, seeking something deep within, and he opens his mouth to say something. But he pauses and looks around the room.

"Did you make dinner?"

Still in my lust-filled haze, I look at Cooper in confusion until I realize that he's carrying me to the kitchen and depositing me on the counter beside the cooled casserole.

"You made this?" he asks as he blindly reaches into the drawer that contains the utensils and grabs a spoon as if he knows exactly where they're located in my kitchen.

"I did."

"Damn," he says around a mouthful of food, not seeming to mind that it's more room temperature than hot. "This is delicious."

"Thanks, I try," I tell him as I make an attempt to hop down from the counter, our moment from a few minutes prior seemingly forgotten, but he stops me with an arm around my waist.

"Where are you going?"

Before I can reply he's shoving a spoonful of the taco casserole into my mouth and I can't help but agree as the flavors spill over my tongue.

For the next ten minutes, I sit on the counter with his arm around my waist as he feeds me in between each of his own bites of food.

"We probably do have to get some actual work done because I have an early day tomorrow."

"Mmhmm," Cooper replies as he sets the spoon in the sink and reaches for a paper towel to wipe his mouth clean. He presses his body between my legs and wastes no time in kissing me again. It's something that I can see myself becoming addicted to so easily. Not just the kisses, but the way he makes me feel when I'm here with him.

Lifting me up as if I weigh nothing more than a feather, he steers us back toward the living room, which surprises me. I would have expected him to head toward the bedroom.

We fall as one onto the cushions, Cooper using his arm to brace me from the fall as I keep my legs wrapped tightly around his hips. He pulls back slightly; his large frame perched just above me as his hand reaches up and moves some hair away from my face.

"How about this? You pick whatever theme you think will work best and then I can spend the rest of the evening worshiping you until you tell me to leave."

"You trust me to pick the theme?"

Finished with the conversation, Cooper bends forward and places his lips at the bottom of my neck. I shiver as he whispers, "Absolutely," against my skin.

"Just kissing, Cooper. I'm not sure I can handle all of you yet."

He chuckles as he places another hot kiss on my neck. "We'll go slow, sweetheart." Sliding down my body he places a kiss just above my chest, "Very," then on my shirt covered navel, "Very," and finally he stops at my bent knee, "Slow."

Cooper begins to work his magic, covering every inch of exposed skin in his searing kisses, leaving my body warm and willing. But he doesn't press me for more, the only pressing he does is with the stiff cock in his pants that he keeps rubbing against my center leaving my panties soaked. I imagine that we look like two horny teenagers going at it when our parents are out. He is proving to be a selfless man, only wanting to taste me and growling every time I pull back to ask if I can explore his body. He claims that the moment I run the show he is going to lose control and kissing won't be all that we do.

I'm unsure how long we've been lying together as he learns my every curve, but when my lips begin to grow numb, I grow the strength to pull my mouth away from his. Sparing a glance at the clock across the wall my eyes expand in size when I note that over an hour has passed since Cooper stepped into my house.

"Do you want me to go?" he asks, and I can see the hope in his eyes shining brightly, the hope that I ask him to stay.

"Well, I can't really feel my lips right now, but we can watch some television if you're up for it."

With the glee that I've only seen on Noah's face when I tell him that he can make slime, Cooper sits up on the couch and tugs me into his side, remote in his hand at the ready. He moves so fast that I'm afraid I'll have a crick in my neck as my head slams against his shoulder. But I won't deny how great it feels to sit here beside him doing something so menial.

"You can watch whatever you like. If you hand me the notebook on the end table, I can start searching through the pictures to see if I like any ideas. I may end up combining some since we've seen the space."

"I don't have any doubts that it will look amazing."

From my perch at his side, I tilt my head to look up at him, surprised to find him glancing down at me. I match his heartwarming smile as I say, "Thank you,

Cooper." And in a move that could easily seal the deal if he were trying to get in my pants tonight, he leans forward and presses those two magnificent lips against my forehead before turning back to watch some game on the television.

Searching through the binder, I take out the sticky tabs Elle tucked into the front folder flap and begin marking items and ideas that I think could work well together. A mix of rustic and modern is what I'm going for, and after about forty-five minutes I think that I have it narrowed down. Sliding my hand across Cooper's waist, I can feel his muscles contract beneath my fingers. Once his attention is on me, I show him the highlights from the notebook and what I plan on having Kerry design for the wedding ceremony and reception. Silence fills my ears and for a moment I question even telling him my thoughts, but without warning, I'm hoisted over his body until I'm deposited on his lap.

"It looks amazing, Sara." He slides his palms up my arms and shoulders until he is cradling my face in his rough hands. "I know that you need to call it a night, but give me five more minutes to continue what we started."

With a gentle but forceful tug, he brings my lips toward his, hovering a smidge away. It takes me a moment, but I realize that he is waiting for me to answer.

"Five more minutes."

Chapter Eight

Cooper

I THOUGHT KISSING SARA a few nights before would have taken the edge off my desire for her, but damn if it didn't just make it about one hundred times more potent. Whenever I find myself lost in thought, my mind is solely focused on remembering the way her lips felt against mine, her soft moans as I'd rub up against her, or the way her skin prickled every time my demanding tongue wanted a taste. I'm finding myself so distracted recently that I almost screwed up in filing some evidence on a case we've been working on.

Since the night at her place, I have been counting down the hours until I get to feel Sara's skin and taste her lips. As I tug on a pair of shorts, I chuckle to myself. All these days I spent being angered and tormented by her, and, of course, equally giving it in return, I had no idea the kind of woman that I was letting slip past me. But not anymore. I plan on taking full advantage of this inch she's given me.

I still wonder what has her so spooked, but we've never spent any time getting to know each other. We went from hate to lust pretty much overnight thanks to the one night she fell asleep on my couch.

Well, today I want to change that. It's a day I've been looking forward to since Elle and Jackson asked for our help – cake tasting day. I'm still surprised Elle didn't want to make the cake herself, but I surmise that she most likely didn't want the stress so close to her big day. Or it could be the fact that something is usually better when someone else does it. Like a massage.

I wonder if Sara would let me give her one, I think to myself as I slip on my shirt and lean down to tie my shoes. I bet every single line of her skin is supple, sweet perfection.

Opening the front door to my house I'm not paying attention as I step onto the porch, but once the door shuts behind me, I look up into the mesmerizing gaze of the woman that's been on my mind for days.

"Hey." I greet her with a smile, so fucking elated to see her beforehand. "I was expecting to see you at the bakery."

"Yeah, I. . .um. . .thought that maybe we could ride together," she admits nervously, her hands twisting in front of her waist and her teeth biting down on the lip that I want to suck into my mouth.

Damn, she's so fucking adorable like this.

Knowing that there are words left unsaid, I press a soft peck against her lips before running my hand through her soft mane of hair. "I couldn't stop thinking about you either, sweetheart."

Sliding my hand from her hair, I trace it down her arm to link our hands together, and that's how we ride in the car and walk into the bakery, our fingers perfectly interlaced as if we're afraid the other may slip away at any moment.

Before we stroll inside, I kiss the tip of her nose, wanting just one more moment with her before I have to give her over to the event planners.

"Hey, want to get some lunch after this?"

With one of those radiant smiles that I'm starting to believe is only reserved for me she replies, "Sure. I was hoping you would ask."

The moment we step through the doors we're assaulted by the trio awaiting our arrival and they usher us over to a small seating area where a table is decorated with the tiniest cakes I have ever seen – two of each kind.

Kerry introduces the baker and lets her point out each of the flavors and their combinations. I didn't realize that there could be so many choices. I only knew of vanilla, chocolate, and maybe red velvet if I wanted to go crazy. But as she points out a pink champagne flavor, I am tossed into a world that I didn't know existed.

As the baker hands us both sheets of paper to mark off the cakes we like and dislike and any comments, she walks off with Kerry and Taylor saying that she is going to gather the batches of icing and filling for us to try as well.

When they walk past Sara, she giggles and grabs the cake closest to her. "You look like you've just walked onto a stage with a full audience and you're completely naked."

"Yeah, that sounds about right."

She giggles again and hands me the same piece of cake she's getting ready to try. "Don't worry, we'll pick something marvelous."

"Whatever you say."

As the group walks back over to our table, a tray of small bowls carried by the baker is set on the now empty table.

"Was there anything that stood out to you?" she asks.

"We've narrowed it down to two. I like the champagne cake," Sara says and then I chime in, "And I like the hazelnut almond."

"Both great choices. So what I have now are fillings that you are welcome to use or not, and different types of icing and flavors. For the hazelnut, I would recommend raspberry filling mixed with chocolate ganache and a mocha buttercream. And for the champagne may I suggest any of the fruit fillings and a simple vanilla buttercream.

"I'll let you two decide what you'd like then we can discuss design. Kerry mentioned that your friend has some ideas of what she'd like?"

"Yes, she's given us a few options and based on the theme we've settled on we're thinking a naked cake, or lightly iced, would look fantastic." Sara reaches into her bag and pulls out a picture she's taken from the notebook. "I'm thinking something like this."

"This will be a great choice for either of the cakes you like. I'll leave you both to sample the icings and fillings and I'll bring out a few more slices of the cake you liked so you can try them together."

"Thank you," Sara and I say simultaneously. A minute or so ticks by until the baker brings out the extra slices of cake and then she leaves to join Kerry and Taylor at another table where they seem to be discussing another event.

"So. . .I'm not really sure I'm going to have room for lunch after all of this. I severely underestimated how much cake we would be tasting."

"Oh thank God, same here. I really want to undo the button on my shorts right now."

A chuckle sounds from my chest as I imagine the straight-laced Sara leaning back in her chair with the button of her shorts undone and her shirt and hair askew. "Maybe we can skip lunch and go grab a drink and head to the park or something."

With a tiny spoon in her hand, Sara swipes some of the filling and icing onto one of the small squares of cake as she says, "That sounds like a good plan."

I follow suit and layer some filling and icing on the morsels of cake, drinking water between each bite. I'm unsure how it happens, but as I am scooping out the last of the raspberry filling the spoon flicks out of my hand and onto the table and I watch in horror as the filling launches off the spoon and right onto Sara's cheek as she is leaning over the table to finish her last bite.

Instead of making a scene or yelling like any of my past flings would have done, Sara looks at me in confusion, and then retaliation. "Did you just flick raspberry filling at me?" she questions without taking a moment to wipe the filling from her cheek.

Holding my hands up innocently I tell her, "It was an accident," but I can tell by the look in her eyes that she doesn't believe me.

"Mmhmm, I just bet it was." Taking a huge scoop of icing into her finger, she reaches across the table and swipes her hand against the side of my face and then smiles gleefully as if she has just won a first place trophy. Too bad she just started a war and I'm the black knight.

Taking my own scoop of icing, I reach out and aim for her cheek, but catch her neck as she tries to turn away. And when she makes her move to stand from the table, I quickly grab her waist and tug her onto my lap where I proceed to cover her cheeks and shoulders in chocolate.

"Children," Kerry grumbles condescendingly standing by the table. "Did you make a decision?"

I look at Sara and she nods. "I think we'll go with the hazelnut, with the blackberry filling and vanilla buttercream."

"Great, I will let the baker know. Now go clean up, you're both a mess. The bathrooms are down that hall." She gestures and then leaves us with our mess.

Sara sneaks into the bathroom first, and I try to slip in with her but she refuses. She pops out a few minutes later looking perfect and I quickly do the same.

"Ready?"

"Sure. There is a frozen lemonade stand we can go to that is close to the park if you're okay with that."

Taking her hand, I kiss the back of the soft skin. "Absolutely."

The park is filled with children running around the jungle gym area and a few runners maneuver around the couples walking around the small lake. Even with the noise of laughter around us, I feel a sense of peace as Sara and I sit with our hands laced between us and our frozen lemonades on the ground at our feet.

"This is nice," she murmurs on a deep sigh. "It's been a long time since I took a day just to relax. I need to make it a point to do this more often."

"Why don't you take time for yourself?" I ask, truly curious of her response.

"I don't know. It all started in college. I wanted to do well, make sure that I earned my scholarships, you know? Then when I went to law school, I was determined to graduate at the top of my class, so I spent every waking moment studying. That's when Elle and I grew apart a bit, but once I graduated, I moved here, which is where she was living. But her business was just starting up, so unless she needed me to watch the kids for her, I just worked on cases during the weekend. That turned into busting my tale for this promotion that I have. Pretty pathetic, huh?"

"Not pathetic, it's not much different than how I was. I willingly took extra shifts or coverage as needed because I didn't have anything better to do. And if I had a weekend free, I'd usually end up at my parents' house and mom would spend her time badgering me about being single."

"Oh, I know all about that. My mom has been on my case for months about settling down. Since Elle and Jackson started dating."

"Well, now you can at least appease her by telling her that we're dating."

"Is that what we're doing? Dating?"

"I only plan on seeing you and taking you out and learning every perfect part of you. So, if you plan on the same, then I would say that we're dating."

Her winning smile tells me that I've answered her in a way that she approves of.

"So, I've always wondered why someone would want to be a divorce lawyer."

"Well, it wasn't my first choice, to be honest. Growing up I had a completely different plan in mind, but I watched my college roommate struggle when her parents divorced after twenty or so years together. And it wasn't so much the divorce on her, it was how it affected her five-year-old sister. The parents were pretty much fighting over the child and it took its toll. So I vowed, especially after my own issues with my parents' divorce, that I would make sure no child goes through what many do."

"But do you like it?"

"My job? I mean, when I help a family separate as amicably as possible it's totally worth it. But for the most part it's a job that pays the bills, very well I might add."

"What would you be doing if you could do anything in the world?"

She reaches down and grabs her lemonade, takes a sip and then looks out toward the jungle gym to the right of us with a dreamlike look on her face. "Most little girls want to be a princess or pretend to be a teacher, but me? I wanted to run a daycare. I wanted to take care of babies and toddlers and help teach them the things to make them happy human beings. It's silly, I know, but until my roommate went through her divorce that was what I wanted to do."

"It's not silly at all. I've seen you with Noah and Kennedy, and you light up when you're with them. What would you have to do to achieve that? Would you have to start from scratch?"

"Not from scratch. I actually have quite a few course credits under my belt if I decided to go back to school, but it's so overwhelming to even consider right now. And I just got that promotion. . .it's crazy to think about. It won't ever happen." Sara shakes her head as she looks down at the concrete walkway before us.

"You can make it happen if that's what you want. I have zero doubts about that."

"I don't know. I think maybe I'm past that part of my life. Why would I want to quit my job just to go back to school again? It's a pipe dream."

"If it's something you want, you should go for it. You could always move in with me. I'll even let you stay rent-free. I'm sure there is some other way you could pay me." I wink in her direction with a sleazy grin on my face and I earn another giggle that I was beginning to crave.

But her laughter quickly turns serious as she leans forward and tilts her head toward me. "You'd do that for me, wouldn't you? Let me upend your life so I can selfishly quit my job."

"It's not selfish at all. And you wouldn't upend my life at all. Just consider it."

"You know, I always had you pegged as this guy sent to this world solely to torment me. I think that maybe I was wrong."

"Oh, but I do like to torment you. It's one of my favorite things."

"You mean like the time at Kennedy's birthday party that you put methylene blue in my drink?"

I burst out in laughter remembering how she left her drink on the table to help divvy out the birthday cake and I slipped a drop into her drink. I can't even remember how I had gotten a hold of the dye.

"Classic."

"Yeah, except for the fact that it had me vomiting all night."

"Oh, yeah. I forgot about that part," I apologize.

"It's okay. Remember I got my payback once you confessed to spiking my drink."

"How can I forget the Ex-Lax brownies that you had Elle make? I still can't take a bite of a brownie without getting shudders."

"And, if we're making confessions, you're definitely not the snooty bitch that I thought you were with your tight buns and suits. You're. . ."

She looks back at me and arches one of her perfectly sculpted brows. "I'm what?"

Grinning at her with a smile I've been told could melt the panties off of a nun, I tell her, "Perfect. You're perfect, Sara." Wrapping my arm around her shoulder, I tug her close and she willingly leans into my body.

"This should be weird," she begins, "but it's not. How in the world did we go from fighting like cats and dogs to ending up here? Like this?"

"I stole your kisses."

"Hmm," she replies as she cuddles closer to me and I catch a waft of fragrance from her hair, a sweet vanilla and honey combination that I want to drown in.

We sit silently for a few moments just watching the families in the park and it's nice to be with her like this. Like we're in our own world with nothing and no one to interrupt.

"So, you know my life story. Tell me, why did you become a cop?"

"Detective," I correct her jokingly. "And I kind of fell into it. I knew that I wanted to serve my country and community, but I knew that I wasn't cut out for the military, at least not when I was younger. I was scrawny as hell and had a temper to make up for what I lacked in muscles. When I graduated college with a degree in criminal justice, I immediately went through the recruitment process at the local department. I liked where I was living. But when Jackson and Hunter came to me about starting the landscaping business on the side as a partner, I made the transfer. It was an easy decision. And frankly, I missed my family.

"Then I got the promotion to detective when the position opened up not long after I moved here. To be honest, until recently, I've been doing regular patrols and my detective work, but we're finally fully staffed which is why I've been able to cut back my hours."

"Is it everything you imagined it would be?"

"I have good days and bad days. But I wouldn't be happy doing anything else."

"It's a risky job though, right?"

"Every job is risky if you think about it. Something could happen to anyone at any time. Maybe a co-worker snaps, or you get in an accident commuting to work."

"That's true. It's just that, now I have a vested interest in the safety of our law enforcement."

"I'll be fine, sweetheart. I'm very careful and I'm always aware of my surroundings. My partner, José, says that I have 360-degree vision. For example, I know that behind me is a woman wearing a pink sweater and she's pushing a stroller that has blue trim."

Sara sits up and looks over her shoulder to see the woman I'm describing and then turns back to me with astonishment in her eyes.

"How did you know that?"

"360."

"Wow," she whispers as she settles back against me. I won't tell her that I pretty much have a photographic memory and can remember what she was wearing the first time I met her. I'll leave that bit of information out of the conversation, it drove my last girlfriend crazy.

"Ready to go back home? I have a surprise for you."

She sits up quickly, the top of her head barely missing my chin.

Clapping her hands Sara bounces in place fueled by her excitement. "Oh, I love surprises."

"Good, I think you're really going to like this one."

Chapter Nine

Sara

SITTING ON COOPER'S COUCH as he throws together a stir-fry for dinner, my nerves start to get the better of me. Staring blankly at his bookshelf I take notice of intricate pieces of paper folded into shapes. Moving toward the shelf, I notice that they are little origami animals and shapes upon further inspection.

"Dinner's ready," Cooper calls out, leaning around the wall.

"Did you make these?" I ask as I hold up a pair of origami shaped lips.

His hand rubs the back of his neck bashfully as he admits to their creation. I'm in awe of these intricate pieces of art that this man has made.

"They're remarkable, Cooper."

"Thanks. Unfortunately, it was an ex that taught me how to create them, but they're a good stress reliever."

Normally the ex part would have had me rolling my eyes, but instead I'm thankful someone was able to share this craft with him.

"Could you teach me?" I ask and his eyes widen in surprise, not expecting me to want to share something with him that he shared with something else.

"Sure. But first, let's eat."

The dinner is delicious, as I expect. Cooper is proving time and time again to be far more than I imagined him to be. He is warm and caring and someone I could easily find myself falling for if that part of me wasn't so closed off. But he is slowly starting to open a fissure in the wall I've built around myself. I only remember one other time where I've felt this way and it happened so fast then disappeared just as quickly, it lives now only in my dreams.

"Hey," Cooper says, drawing my attention away from my stare at the tabletop. I look up to find him holding a stack of square paper. "Did you still want to learn?"

Jumping from the chair, I eagerly bypass him and head to the living room. I've always been a person that is enthusiastic to learn new things.

When Cooper joins me, I'm sitting on the floor in front of his coffee table ready to be taught. He smiles as he takes a seat on the floor next to me and lays out a few pieces of thin paper.

"Which shape did you want to start off with?"

"Oh, um. . ." I consider, tapping my finger on my chin. "The kiss."

I follow his directions and do my best to fold my piece of paper in the same manner as Cooper, but somewhere along the way, my kiss looks more like a folded triangle.

Blowing out a puff of air I pout, "I don't know what I did wrong."

Cooper chuckles as he sets his creation aside and grabs a new piece of paper. Crawling on his knees he moves behind me then cradles my body between his legs, his arms on either side of me.

"Let's try again," Cooper suggests as he hands me the paper then rests his hands on top of mine.

Slowly he guides my every movement, directing my fingers through every fold of the delicate paper, until finally, I have a perfect kiss resting in my hands.

"I did it! Oh my gosh, now show me how to do the star!" I request gleefully, and following the same manner, Cooper helps me to create a beautiful three-dimensional star.

"Okay, I want to try one by myself."

"Go ahead," Cooper proposes, wrapping his arms around my waist at the same time that he presses a kiss against the back of my neck.

I'm so lost in the folds of the paper and remembering each of the steps that I don't realize Cooper has been running his hands up and down my back. But as he starts to knead the muscles around my shoulders, I lose my concentration and sink back against him. A moan releases from my chest uncontrollably, the noise sounding foreign to even my own ears.

"I would pay you to do this for hours."

Adjusting his hands, he begins working the muscles around my neck and shoulders, ripping another moan from me.

"I would do it for free. Do you want one?"

I would be an absolute fool to turn down a massage from a handsome man. I've only had a professional massage once before in my life and it was a terrible experience that left me sore for days. I'm not sure what went wrong, but it isn't something that I had ever planned on repeating. But never once during that session did it feel anywhere close to how Cooper is making my body feel. I'm so relaxed from just a few gentle rubs on my back that I could curl up in a ball and go to sleep.

Moving his body with the grace of a dancer, not like I would have imagined a large muscled man to move, he stands and grabs my hand, tugging me up from the floor. With slow steps he guides me down the hall to what I am assuming is his bedroom. He doesn't want me to think he is being presumptuous, his slow steps give me every opportunity to retreat. But I don't want to pull away, I want to take this chance with him, even if it is nothing more than him working the muscles on my back.

Tenderly he guides me to the end of the bed and kisses me before taking a step back.

"I think I have some candles around here. Let me go find them," he suggests, but before he can pull away, I shake my head.

"Cooper, it's fine."

"Are you sure? I want you as relaxed as possible."

I attempt to lighten the mood that seems to weigh heavy in the room. "Why, so you can take advantage of me?"

It takes a second, but he finally relaxes and grins back down at me. I wouldn't have ever imagined that being alone with me in his bedroom would make Cooper feel nervous. With how attractive he is I would think he's used to having women here with him. Which is not something I want to think further about.

"It's going to sound like a line, but you're the first woman I've brought here."

"Cooper, I've been at Elle's house when you've had women over. Their screams haunt my dreams," I jest, as I push at his chest, but instead of hanging his head in remorse for his lie, the corner of his lips tilt upward in a sexy grin that immediately causes my stomach to flutter wildly.

"Sweetheart, I've only ever allowed other women into my guestroom, never this room. I promise you that you're the first."

"Why?" I whisper.

Leaning down he presses a kiss to my lips. "Because you're special. Now lie down."

Reaching down I grip the edge of my shirt and pull it over my head revealing the red lace bra firmly encasing my breasts. The breasts that Cooper's heated gaze is locked on. When I dressed this morning, I wasn't sure how this day would go, how I would feel when I saw him this morning. Would I still want him with that same passion from earlier in the week? Would that connection we have still burn as brightly? Would I still want to risk myself getting hurt for a chance to feel desired?

As I tug open my shorts and let them pool at my feet revealing the matching lace panties, I immediately know that I made the right choice to be here in this moment with Cooper.

"Christ, are you trying to kill me? I think I'm having a heart attack." His hand rests on his chest.

"No, I just thought this would make it easier."

"Maybe for you," he counters as he gestures with his eyes to the erection behind his shorts. "Go ahead and lie down. I'm going to grab some lotion."

Nodding, I turn around and crawl across the bed, grab a pillow, then settle against the gray duvet. With Cooper out of the room, I take a minute to look around the room. It's another space his mother must have decorated. Most of the palette is a mix of black, whites, and grays, but touches of bronze are scattered throughout. It should feel cold and unwelcoming, but it's the opposite and I feel a sense of peace in the room.

"Alright," Cooper announces as he comes back carrying a bottle of lotion in one hand and a towel in the other. "So, what kind of massage would you like? Anywhere in particular that you'd like me to focus on?"

"You can do whatever you'd like, Cooper."

"Are you sure about that?" he asks as he slowly trails the tips of one hand up the inside of one leg. From my ankle to my thigh he leaves a path of fire in his wake, and when he approaches the apex of my thighs, he brazenly runs his fingers across the center of my panties. My core clenches at the lightest of his touches.

I know now that there is no turning back; I want this with him – tonight.

"Yes, I am."

"Great," he says joyfully, pulling his hand away from my body, the sexy voice from earlier quickly replaced.

He asks if he can unhook my bra, which I oblige willingly, and he slides the straps down my arms. It's only once I settle back onto the pillow that I realize my mistake. A mistake that I haven't considered in years, but will inevitably cause questions.

My heart begins to pound in my chest as I wait in anticipation for the moment to come. The massage that should have relaxed me instead is causing my anxiety to rise.

Should I just point it out before he asks?

"Cooper," I start, wanting to get his attention as his hands travel down my lower back to the spot in question.

"Sara?" he poses, trailing his hand over the jagged scar on my hip. The scar that came from being shoved into a glass coffee table by one of my mother's many suitors when I was in high school. The scar that needed stitches but my mother was at work and the asshole wasn't going to take me to the hospital, so I patched it up myself with butterfly Band-Aids.

Most days I can cover it with my clothing, and when I buy bathing suits, I am always conscious of making sure the red marking is covered. Men never noticed when I'm was intimate with them, they are too focused on the endgame at that point. But now I have no escape.

I lick my lips preparing to delve into the entire story, thoughts I would rather not rehash, but Cooper continues, "Holy, fuck. I can't believe it's you."

Confused, I grab the towel resting beside me on the bed and cover my breasts as I turn over, Cooper moving off of me at the same time so that I can sit up.

"What's me?"

"You're the girl from the frat house."

My heart that was already beating in overtime revs up into overdrive. My memories that had turned themselves into dreams flash behind my eyes and I'm left almost gasping for air.

"The boy? The one that told me to get out?"

"Shit, Sara. I went to Raleigh for college and that is where I had my first job. We were there to bust the house because the frat had been running a prostitution and drug ring. I was there to gather evidence.

"Even in the darkness of that basement, you stood out amongst all of the bodies in that room. I had to be close to you. I could barely see two inches in front of me and I'm not sure if I moved on my own or my feet carried me on their free will, but the moment I touched you I was gone.

"I knew I was breaking the rules telling you to get out of there, but I had this overwhelming need to protect you.

"You were wearing this short denim skirt. I remember it so vividly because I was pretty sure that it was made solely to torture me. When I danced with you and my hand ran across your exposed hip I felt this scar," he tells me as he reaches out and runs his finger across the skin at my hip as if he can't control himself. "I wanted to know what happened and why you were left with such an ugly reminder of something. I feel like I was connected to you from that moment on.

"And the strangest part is that when we were introduced, I had asked Jackson if we had possibly met before because there was something about you that seemed so familiar."

"Cooper. . .I. . ." I stumble across the words, unsure of what to say to him, of how to explain.

"I'm sorry, that is probably a lot to take in." With a reserved smile, he looks down at the bed, pulling his brilliant blue eyes from me.

And that won't do.

Dropping the towel, I eagerly climb onto his lap, my bare breasts pressing against the soft cotton of his shirt. As he looks up at me in surprise, I kiss him with every ounce of passion that I have. This man has thought about me for years the same way I thought about my stranger. My stranger that turns out to be this beautiful man.

Pulling my mouth away, I rest both of my hands on his cheeks, the stubble on his jawline feeling soft against my palms. "I have dreamed about that moment for years, Cooper. Years. It's etched so deeply into my mind that I began to think that it was a memory that I made up on my own.

"That first moment your hand touched my skin it seared me. I burned for this man that was a stranger for so long. I wished all the time that I had turned around to see you, but I didn't want to break the moment. Or worse, be disappointed.

"It's stupid, I know, but I was young and had just made major changes in my life. I had sworn that very day that I wasn't going to ever put myself in a position to be hurt the way my mother had been or like all of the families I had witnessed over the years. I didn't want to be disappointed that you were this perfect person that I couldn't have.

"So I gave myself the memory and for the longest time it stayed tucked away in a safe place almost to the point that I forgot everything that happened, but never the feeling. I knew that feeling was something I would never experience again, until Elle and I saw you and Jackson at that restaurant a year ago. I told Elle that I thought I recognized you from somewhere."

"Damn, baby. You know what this means right?"

"What's that?"

"That you're mine, sweetheart."

He doesn't give me a chance to speak. Instead he presses his lips against mine and this time it's different. It's as if a part of Cooper has been unleashed at the knowledge that I'm his mystery woman that he connected with years ago.

Together, as if one, we lie on the bed, Cooper's strong body resting above mine. But it's the moment when he settles himself between my legs that the panic starts to rise. My fear of being hurt, of being broken.

"Cooper, what if I'm still not ready for more than this?"

"Hey, nothing has changed, Sara. If you're not ready for a relationship, then we'll go slow." His declaration eases some of my apprehension. "But just know that I won't let you go without a fight. Fate has brought us together more than once. It's not something I plan on ignoring."

Reaching up I weave my hand through his dark blond hair, loving the feel of the strands as they slide through my fingers.

"I want you, Cooper," I whisper.

"Good, because after everything we just learned if I didn't have you right now, I'm pretty positive that I would explode."

We lie together, our lips sealed as one and my almost naked body under his clothed one. His hand travels up and down my rib cage, just a breath away from my breast. My nipples stand at attention for him, seeking his touch. And finally, after a few agonizing minutes, he pulls away from my mouth and focuses his concentration on my hardened peaks.

Gazing at me with his large hand cupping my breast he says, "Your tits are perfection. The perfect size and so sweet."

"Less talking, more tasting."

"Yes, ma'am."

The obedient man shifts his attention to the ignored breast and immediately begins sucking on the nipple as if it's his dying wish.

"Cooper," I groan as I shift my hips against him. My lower half is awake and needy, wanting his focus. Who am I to deny myself?

"Need me somewhere else, sweetheart? Where do you want me now?"

Rocking my hips against his shorts covered erection, I try to wordlessly get my point across, but the stubborn man shakes his head as he presses a kiss to my navel.

"I need to hear you say it. Tell me where you want me."

"Cooper," I growl, but he simply continues to stare at me waiting.

"Fine. I want you to focus on my pussy, and it better be fucking phenomenal because I hate that word."

If it was possible, Cooper's grin grows two times bigger than I've ever seen as he slides my panties down my legs, tossing them over his shoulder into oblivion.

"Don't worry, sweetheart. I'm going to have you screaming my name in no time."

"Promises. Promises."

I shouldn't doubt Cooper. Ever. Because not even two minutes into his fingers and tongue working their magic on my clit and pussy I'm coming apart at his command. My legs tremble on either side of his body as I struggle to come back into myself.

"You're delicious. I could eat you for breakfast, lunch, and dinner."

"If you can make me come this quickly every time then I can absolutely oblige you. Now, get naked. It's not fair that you still have your clothes on."

"I didn't want the distraction, because if my cock came anywhere close to your pussy, it was going to act selfishly."

"Well, now I'm acting selfishly. Get. Naked," I demand as I tug on his shirt in an attempt to lift it over his head.

Agonizingly slow, Cooper moves off the bed and stands to his full height. I'm not sure how men learned to do it, or realized that it's one of the sexiest ways to remove clothing, but he reaches behind his head with both arms and bunches the back of his shirt in his hands before lifting it over his head. His muscles flex with the movement and I take my time savoring the expanse of bare skin before me.

Crawling onto my knees, I lift my hands onto his shoulders then slide them down his chest, his pectoral muscles contracting under my touch. I repeat the motion down his abdomen, my fingers sliding in and out of the crevices of his defined abs. He throws his head back and groans when I reach the waistband of his shorts, the tips of my fingers sliding just past the material.

The button of his shorts pops open easily as if it also was waiting for my touch. Skimming my hands to his backside, I push down his shorts and boxers in one movement with his assistance. His cock springs free and it is as glorious as I had imagined. Long and thick and stiff. So fucking stiff.

Timidly I reach out and wrap my hand around the base of his shaft, noting how soft the skin is. A complete contrast to the firmness of his erection. My hand slides up and down, learning, discovering. A bead of moisture sits on the tip of his cock and I boldly lean down and lick it away. The saltiness in my mouth is not completely unwelcome. He tastes just as good as he looks.

Wanting to savor more of him, I guide the tip of his erection into my mouth and let the weight of it rest on my tongue before I swirl it around the head. Working my hands in unison with my mouth, I slide him in and out of my lips, the moisture from my mouth allowing my hand to mimic the same movement on his shaft.

Blow jobs have never been one of my favorite parts of foreplay, but with Cooper, I find myself never wanting it to stop. Watching him writhe as I work him over in my mouth is an addictive sight to behold.

With my free hand, I reach between my legs, gliding my fingers through the pool of moisture at the apex of my thighs.

"Fuck, yes. Touch yourself, baby," Cooper demands as he snakes his hand into my hair, taking control of my movements. He doesn't push for more, he simply increases the speed of his thrusts into my mouth.

My finger swirls around my clit, hungry for more. Pulling my mouth free from his cock I look up at Cooper with a begging plea. "I need more, Cooper."

"Fuck, I thought you'd never ask."

In a flash, I'm flipped from my knees onto my back and Cooper is above me kicking himself free from his shorts. I rub myself against him, craving to feel him deep inside me, to have him mark me. His shaft glides against my clit over and over again and I can feel the waves of pleasure building in my core.

"Baby, I need to put on a condom."

I bob my head and he stretches above me and leans over to reach into the nightstand to grab a box that he tosses on the bed beside us. In a practiced move, he tears apart the wrapper with his teeth and fingers and easily covers himself in the latex.

"Are you ready?" he asks, and I nod, my hesitation from earlier easily forgotten.

He aligns himself at my entrance and slowly slips inside, inch by fucking amazing inch.

"You're so fucking tight, baby. God, I could stay in you all night," he explains as he thrusts himself to the hilt.

"Yes," I moan.

He's slow at first, allowing me to adjust to his size but it's not long until we're both frantically matching each other's thrusts. I sink my nails into the skin of his ass cheek when his cock begins to rub against a particularly sensitive spot that has me feeling something I've never felt before. And it's incredible.

Knowing that I must be close to a release, Cooper slides his hand from the breast he had been caressing up to my neck. The hold isn't overly tight, but it's enough to heighten my senses. Every ounce of pleasure I had been experiencing explodes within me as I reach my pinnacle.

Cooper's movements slow down as I come back to myself and he asks if that was okay. But in my glorious haze, I can only mumble, "So good," and nod.

"Good. Now I want to fuck you and watch that magnificent ass."

Flipping my languid body over, he reaches for my hips and jerks them in the air. His erection easily slides back inside my channel, where it belongs, and his thrusts begin again. I rock back against him, the new position allowing his cock to rub against that same sensitive spot.

"That's it, baby. I can feel your pussy squeezing me so tight."

Normally I'm not one for dirty talk, but I could come from Cooper's voice alone. It's hot and wicked, and I want more.

His movements become more frantic, less steady but more powerful, as he gets closer to his release. One of his hands remains on my hip while the other reaches into my hair and tightens it in his fist. At first, it's painful but as I reach my climax I no longer feel the pain. It's not much longer before Cooper releases himself and we fall as one onto the bed in a heap.

"That was. . ." I say, unable to fully describe how amazing the sex was. But it was more than that. It was the day, the new revelations, the feelings.

"It was," he replies as he presses a kiss to my nose and then moves to remove the condom. Wrapping it in a knot, he then tosses it in the trashcan in the corner.

Reaching over, he pulls the corner of the duvet over my body, his arm wrapped around me holding me close.

I smile in thanks, but I'm alarmed when I sense a feeling of vulnerability coming from him.

"Sara?"

"Yeah?"

"Would you stay?"

He's asking me to stay the night, but for some reason, I feel as if there is an underlying meaning to his question. But I surprise myself when I decide not to think about it.

"Okay."

And if I could be the recipient of that answering smile every day, then I have no doubts that I could fall for this man.

Chapter Ten

Cooper

I WAS NEVER THE man that needed a relationship or sex to be happy. I was content going to my job, coming home to my dog, and being with my family. But that all changed when Sara barged into my life. She knocked me on my ass and I found myself wanting to spend every moment with her.

Unfortunately for me, Sara and I are finding that navigating this new relationship of ours is going to be harder than we imagined. It would probably help if she'd acknowledge the fact that we are in a relationship at all and not just having sex. As amazing as the sex is, I'm ready for more. I've already come to terms with the fact that the woman I wanted to strangle senseless whenever she was near me is now the woman that I want to fuck senseless. She just needs time and I've promised her that.

But damn if it doesn't suck. I'm not usually a patient man, wanting to feel the surge of satisfaction as soon as possible, but for Sara, I am going to try.

Tonight we have agreed to host separate bachelor and bachelorette parties for Elle and Jackson, despite both of them remaining stoic in their stance that they don't want one. But Sara and I have promised them that we will keep it low-key. Or in layman terms – no strippers. I'm not sure what Sara has planned for Elle, but I'm going to host a poker game for Jackson and invite our cousin Hunter, our dad, and a few of Jackson's friends from work. I'm keeping my fingers crossed that Sara's brother declines the invite. He would kick my ass if he knew I was fucking his sister. And I'm big, but he is massive and could crush me with just his finger. I'm hoping that since he was pining away for Elle that it may be awkward for him to be here to celebrate Jackson getting the girl.

But if he does show maybe I can pick his brain for why his sister remains so closed off. She gives a little more of herself every time that we're together, but I want it all.

Last night she canceled our standing date and time in the bedroom without giving a reason. And I shouldn't have been disappointed, but I was. Lying here in my empty bed, sheets cold beside me, I realize how far gone I am for this girl, and we've only been together for a couple of weeks, most of that being spent apart. But even though I slept alone, Sara wasn't far from my thoughts. For the first time in years I didn't dream of the mysterious woman in the dark frat house basement, I dreamt of Sara. The skin I touched in vain was Sara's. The sweat soaked hair that brushed against my chest was Sara's soft strands. My mind pieced the two women into one, how they should be. It was a seamless transition. I can only hope that it's as easy for Sara to put me in place of the man in her memory.

Sighing, I drag myself out of bed and step into the shower, the initial coolness of the water waking me up just as the sun begins to crest over the trees in my backyard.

Lathering my body with soap, I close my eyes as I reach down and stroke my cock, the stiff shaft hardening further when an image of Sara from last weekend comes into view. Her tanned skin glimmering in the moonlight cast through the window. Her supple breasts with their rose-colored peaks begging me for attention. And the folds of her sweet pussy glistening with her own desire. She was a masterpiece from the heavens sent to me to fulfill every one of her fantasies and mine.

Remembering how she shuddered in my arms as she fell apart by my tongue, my balls tighten and I expel my own release into my palm. Reaching out I rest one hand on the wall of my shower and follow suit with my forehead, the cool tile feeling luxurious against my heated skin. This woman has me so worked up just thinking about her.

"Fuck it," I whisper to myself as I step out of the shower, grabbing my towel hanging from the rod behind the door and dry myself off.

Without a second thought, I tug on a pair of boxers and jeans, blindly grab a T-shirt from my dresser and slip it over my head and down my chest, then throw on some socks and sneakers. I rush through my routine in the bathroom, brushing my teeth and swirling mouthwash eagerly in my mouth. Running my hands through my hair with a little gel gives it the look that I know women go crazy for, as I've been told a number of times, and I head to the kitchen.

Once Bailey is taken care of, I grab a protein bar and head out the door with one destination in mind. Sara doesn't get to cancel on me without an explanation. So unless she's dying from bird flu, she better be prepared to explain herself.

And if I don't get my hands on her as soon as possible, I might very well go crazy. A week is too long to go without seeing her. We need to fix this, now.

I realize my mistake as soon as I knock on Sara's door. The screaming coming from the other side has me taking a step back. And then another. I'm hoping that I can sneak away before Sara opens the door, but just as I turn to take the stairs, the screaming intensifies as her door opens.

"Cooper?" her musical voice says from behind me and I turn sheepishly. "What are you doing here?"

"Uncle Cooper?" a young voice sounds from the room, the screaming immediately halting, much to the delight of Sara's neighbors I'm sure.

"Hey, Noah. I just came by to see your Aunt Sara, but I can see that you guys are busy."

Noah steps from around Sara's bare legs and chimes, "We're having a sing-along party."

Oh, well that explains the screaming.

"Want to play?" Kennedy asks as she joins her brother.

"Uh. . . sure."

This isn't how I expected to spend my morning, but if it gives me time with Sara, then I'll sacrifice his hearing for a few hours.

I watch as Noah and Kennedy scurry away and then put my focus back to the woman leaning against the doorjamb with her arms crossed against her chest and a saucy smirk.

"You came here to call me out for canceling last night, didn't you?" she asks as if she doesn't already know the answer to that question. "Elle's mom was supposed to watch the kids last night, just like your mom is watching the kids tonight. But she canceled last minute, and Elle didn't have a backup. She asked me if I could take the rugrats so she could finish up a big order so she could be free tonight. Of course, I said yes."

Nodding I step closer to her without saying a word, watching as the smirk slips from her face. I move into her space, sliding a hand across her cheek and into her hair. Her head tilts up toward mine, bringing our lips closer.

"I missed you last night. I've missed you every night," I tell her.

Whispering her reply she says, "I missed you too, Cooper." She uncrosses her arms and rests her hands on my waist, the skin beneath her palms tingling under her touch. Rising onto the tips of her feet Sara presses her lips against mine, and every ounce of irritation I was feeling this morning fizzles away into oblivion. She is the calm to my storm.

"Uncle Cooper," Noah shouts from behind us and I pull our lips apart, only to press another peck on the corner of her mouth.

"We're going to talk later. But first I have some eardrums to burst."

The kids are bouncing around the room, jumping from the couch, to a chair, then onto the floor, only to repeat the process again. After a few minutes of watching them sing along to a few Disney melodies, Sara finally convinces them that it's quiet time and to go sit in their room and play. I'm surprised when the kids don't even argue or throw a temper tantrum. They wordlessly move into Sara's guest bedroom and make themselves absent.

Sara takes a seat beside me on the couch, her thigh pressing against mine, and I can't help but reach out and rest my hand on the exposed skin.

"You could have just told me that you were watching the kids. I would have come over to help you. I like spending time with them."

Her doe eyes cast downward matching the direction of the corner of her lips. Regret pours off Sara in waves. "I wasn't thinking. I'm not used to having someone else to rely on or to have to explain myself to. It never occurred to me that you would care. I mean, it's just sex, right?" she reiterates as she turns her gaze toward me.

"Maybe for you," I tell her honestly.

She turns on the couch and tucks one of her feet under the opposite leg. "Cooper, I. . .Oh. My. Gosh," she says in horror as her hand flies over her mouth as she looks at the place where the hallway meets the living room.

"What?" I ask as I turn to see whatever she is looking at. "Are those?"

"Yes," she whispers laughs.

Kennedy stands proudly before us, anal beads draped around her neck, and, what I believe are cock rings, dangling from her wrists.

"This is a funny sword, Aunt Sara," Noah calls out as he walks into the living room carrying a large black dildo in his hand and a smaller pink one in the other. "I brought you a sword, Uncle Cooper. Can we play knights, please?"

The little devil tries to hand me the pink dildo, and I balk away from it as I look to Sara for help. Shouldn't she be mortified that the kids have found her stash of playthings? Instead of embarrassment covering her face, she is wiping away tears from laughter.

"Kids, please go put those back where you got them from. Those are not toys for you to play with," Sara demands through peals of laughter. I can see that she is trying to keep it together but is failing miserably.

As the kids sulk back to the room, their cherub faces crestfallen, I turn to Sara wanting an explanation.

"They were for the bachelorette party tonight. It's a toy party."

In horror, I jump from the couch and begin to pace. "A toy party? What if my mother was here?"

"Who do you think gave me the idea? I actually think she's going to see if your aunt wouldn't mind watching the kids so that she can come. She is supposed to let me know this morning."

"Oh no, my mother does not know anything about sex toys. Or about sex, for that matter."

She laughs which only angers me further. "How do you think you and Jackson got here, Cooper?"

"Immaculate conception!"

"Don't be delusional. I think it's amazing that your parents have a healthy sex life at their age."

Pushing my hands against my ears I do my best to ignore her, but it does no good. It only causes her to laugh again. "Stop talking about it, Sara."

"Why? I should ask your mom what toy she likes best," the devil woman says as she pulls out her phone and begins typing out a message. My feet carry me as quickly as possible across the room, jumping over the coffee table in my haste to stop her from messaging my mother.

I land on top of her, pressing her body onto the couch cushions. She holds the phone in her hand above her head, trying to keep it out of my reach, but she's unsuccessful. I rip the phone away and toss it onto the chair on the other side of the room.

"Hey!" she protests, her arms reaching for my chest in an attempt to push me off, but I'm not budging.

"Why would you torture me like this?"

"Because it was funny. I wasn't really texting your mom, that would be a little weird. But it really was her idea for the party."

"Please stop talking now."

"Make me," the saucy vixen taunts.

Sealing our lips together, I keep her quiet in the best way possible. My tongue licks at her lips, begging for entrance, and she willingly obliges its plea.

"Ew," a small voice sounds from the corner. "They're playing that game that mommy and daddy play a lot. Let's go back to our room."

I kiss her as if I'm not aware of the duo in the other room, but it's not enough. I want so much more. Fueled by her taste, I slide my hand between our bodies and slip it past the top of her shorts and panties. Her bare mound surprises me, since the last time we were together she had been delicately trimmed between her legs, but my mind isn't on her shaving preference. I'm far more interested in the slick folds that my fingers are running through.

"Cooper," she moans against my mouth. It's a plea to stop and to continue. I follow the latter as her hips rock against my hand, her greedy pussy sucking my finger into its tight channel.

"Fuck my hand, baby. Take what you want." She moves against the heel of my palm which rests against her small bundle of nerves. "That's it, sweetheart. I can feel your pussy gripping my finger." Her channel begins to tighten and I know she's about to fall apart at my hand. "Let go, baby."

Covering her mouth with my own, I rock my hand against her clit and increase the thrust of my fingers. It takes another minute, her body fighting against its own climax, but she finally falls apart and I swallow her cries of pleasure.

"Oh my gosh, I cannot believe that we just did that," she whispers in a horrified expression, but I can hear the tiniest bit of thrill in her voice even as she tries to cover it.

"Dirty girl. I can't believe you took advantage of me when you're watching the kids. Goodness, what would Elle think?"

She shoves me aside with a snarky laugh and adjusts her clothing.

"Elle would laugh because I know for a fact that quiet time for the kids means sexy time for her and Jackson."

"Well, that would explain the kids walking in and then right back out."

I watch in amusement as the blood drains from her face.

"What?"

"Yeah, they said something about playing a game like Mom and Dad and walked back out."

"How did I miss that?"

"You were too lost in all of the amazing things I was doing to your body."

"Yeah, yeah, Casanova." Sara stands from the couch still trying to adjust her shorts to her liking but gives up with a huff and decides to run her fingers through her hair instead. "If you're going to hang around for the day do you mind if I go take a shower?"

"That's fine. I'll watch the heathens. Even though you know, you could just move in with me, and we can conserve water by showering together."

Turning her back toward me she sways those magnificent hips as she walks down the hall.

"Baby steps, Cooper. Baby steps."

Taking in my living room, I've moved the coffee table out of the way and set up a card table and a cooler in front of my fireplace and I have a Pay-Per-View boxing match playing in the background. As much as I wish we could have taken Jackson to a strip club for a standard bachelor party, I know he would have hated it. That man has been blind to everyone since Elle moved next door to him. Even when he complained on a daily basis about her. They're not too dissimilar from myself and Sara now that I think about it.

A knock on the door sounds and my father and Hunter walk in, each carrying a case of their favorite beer. I offered to have everyone crash at my place tonight so that they were able to indulge a bit more than normal. After shaking hands and man-hugging my father I repeat it with Hunter, we're a very affectionate bunch. I take their beer and put it in the iced cooler for later. My dad, Stan, immediately heads toward the chips and salsa I bought from a local Mexican restaurant on the way home along with the fixings for a taco bar.

Not long after my family arrives a few of Jackson's trainers from his gym and some of our hired landscapers join the party. We're just waiting on the man of the hour.

"If you guys want to get your food, I'll go check on Jackson," I tell them and watch as they eagerly rush to my kitchen.

Stepping out onto my porch I look over at the house next door and its outside lights shining brightly across the yard. The lights are out inside the house, the blackness meshing with the darkness outside. I turn to go back inside and grab my phone and that's when I see it. A couple pressed against the hood of an SUV going at it like a bunch of teenagers. The man fists the woman's bottom as she paws at his back, their mouths fused into one.

"Okay, please stop before I see more of you than I ever need to," I shout, causing Jackson to drop Elle from his grasp. She lands with a thump onto the front bumper of her car and mutters a curse. "Now, get to my house for your party you bastard and let Elle go to hers."

"Fine," Jackson mumbles as he kisses Elle once more and smacks her ass as she moves to enter her SUV.

As my brother walks past me, I hear him grumble, "I hate you." So, I kindly reply, "I know," and follow him into my house.

The group is collectively shoving all of the food into their mouths as quickly as possible when I stroll back into my kitchen. I'm glad that I had the forethought to hide a few extra servings that I can toss in the oven for later.

"Alright, who wants to lose some money?" my dad calls out as he takes his plate to the card table.

"You wish, old man," Hunter jokes as he follows suit, the rest of the guys leaving the kitchen with their plates and finding a seat at the table.

Just as I fix up a plate for myself, a knock sounds on the front door and I carry my half-made plate to answer. As I open the door, I'm actually surprised to see the person standing on the other side.

"Aiden, hey. Come on in." I extend my free hand to Sara's brother who is standing a few inches taller than me with about twenty pounds more of muscle and he shakes it roughly before grabbing the plate from my hand.

"Thanks for the invite. . .and the plate," he adds as he takes the taco and shoves it in his mouth while walking past me and heading to the group of guys in the living room. If it were anyone else I would have something to say about the bastard stealing my dinner, but he's Sara's brother, and I'm going to be walking a fine line for the rest of the evening.

"Come take a seat, son," my father calls out from the living room and I tell him that I'll be just a moment as I get set at making another plate.

We play a few rounds of poker, most of the group watching the match on the television, but once the big fight is over, we all start our ribbing on Jackson for taking the leap and getting hitched.

"Man, when you go all in you really go all in. Wife and kids all in one swoop," one of the gym trainers points out.

"Hey, I can't help that I was handed the perfect package right next door," Jackson replies, tossing a piece of chip in the direction of the guy I barely know.

Beside me, I hear Aiden mutter under his breath, "Stole that fucking perfect package."

Hearing that from Sara's brother alarms me. I realize that Sara had joked that he had a crush on Elle, but I never considered that maybe it was more than just a crush to him. And now my hackles rise.

Reaching out I grab Aiden's arm to grab his attention and whisper, "You're not going to be a problem are you?" And I'm actually surprised to see a hint of fear in Aiden's eyes and that's when I remember that he is young, much younger than my thirty-three years.

"No way. I want Elle to be happy. You don't have to worry." I stare him down for a moment then allow him to shake off my hand. Hopefully, I've gotten my point across that nothing will come between my brother and his happiness. Or Elle's because I already love her like a sister.

"Good," I reply and then turn my attention back to the card game starting up again.

Surprising us all, my father is holding the majority of the chips. Who knew that my father was such a card shark? Most of the guys have loosened up past the point of a buzz and now are actively heading toward the point of no return.

As Jackson shoves a few chips into his mouth and folds another set of cards, I turn to my drunk brother with a stone-cold face, mainly because I haven't had a lick to drink.

"So, man, are you ready? Nervous at all?"

"No way. I don't care if you and Sara decide to have us walk down the aisle riding flamingos and then dancing the funky chicken after our vows. I just want to be married to her."

From beside me, Aiden sits up as if finally paying attention to everything going around outside of stealing his chips back from my father. "What do you mean 'You and Sara'?"

Casually Jackson explains how he and Elle asked us to plan the details of their wedding while they finish their busy season and training of their staff.

With an inquisitive eye and a straight back, Aiden turns to me and eyes me up and down, a move I've pulled on one too many criminals. "You're spending time with my sister?"

I take a healthy gulp from my glass of water as I mentally try to explain the situation without giving away any details Sara's brother definitely doesn't need to know. "Just Saturdays with the event planner and an evening here and there when we've been assigned homework. Dude, it's like we've been assigned a group project in school."

Something in my chest pulls as I lessen whatever it is that Sara and I are doing when I speak to her brother. She's more than just a few days-a-month partner, far more than I'm letting on. But I don't want to make things difficult for her, or for me.

"That better be all it is," Aiden mumbles under his breath as he takes a swig of his beer and then gets up and heads down the hall toward the bathroom.

With my neighbor gone I reach into my back pocket and grab my phone, I have an uncontrollable desire to reach out to Sara, strictly to see if she is having fun with her friends. I unlock the screen and see that I have a missed text message from about ten minutes ago. A message from the woman currently invading my thoughts.

I try to mask the smile on my face as I turn to the guys and toss down my cards.

"Sorry, guys. I just got called in to check over a current arrest related to a case I'm handling. Dad, make sure no one leaves, or drinks all of my beer," I command as I stand from the table and grab my leather jacket and helmet from the hook by the door.

"You got it, kid," my dad says as he looks up at me. I don't miss the wink in his eye and I instantly know that he knows that I'm not going to the office. I can only hope that he doesn't let anyone know what he suspects. . .or who.

Chapter Eleven

Sara

ELLE IS HAPPILY DRUNK on my couch holding her personal bottle of pink champagne while a few of our friends sit scattered around the room as Magic Mike plays on the television. The toy party was a hit, as I expected. I almost wish that Naomi, Cooper and Jackson's mom, had been able to make it since it was her idea, but her sister wasn't able to watch her soon-to-be grandchildren after all. But I made sure to send her plenty of pictures.

As the girls veg out watching Channing Tatum grind on the stage, I send a text to Cooper asking how his night is going then start to tidy up the mess that we made. Between the dinner, snacks, and plastic packages I fill up an entire trash bag just as the movie comes to a close on the screen. I glance over the counter looking out into the living room and find the women passed out with dreamy smiles on their faces. None brighter than Elle's and I know that it's not Channing Tatum she's dreaming of, but it's Jackson. I consider waking them up to head to the bedrooms to sleep more comfortably, but then I decide against it.

Making sure to grab my keys I take the trash bag and lock the door on my way out, just to be on the safe side with my friends sleeping inside, and make my way to the dumpster. It's dark out, one of the lights behind the condo complex blinking as it struggles to stay lit. As quickly as I can I scurry toward the community dumpster and with a heave, I toss the bag into the oversized barrel listening as the trash thumps against the metal.

A shiver climbs up my spine causing the tiny hairs at the base of my neck to stand on end. It's a feeling that I don't welcome. Spinning on my heels I walk quickly, my hands tightened into fists as my arms hang tensely by my sides.

I'm so focused on getting back into my condo that I don't notice the man standing against the wall watching me, waiting for me. The shadow reaches out, a strong arm wrapping around my waist, and tugs me closely.

A shriek escapes my throat but a hand clamps over my mouth to silence me. My panic rises, but as the figure pulls me against his hard body and I catch his signature male scent, I instantly relax. And then turn in his arms to swat his shoulder.

"Why would you scare me like that?" I accuse.

"I'm sorry, baby. I thought that you knew it was me."

"It's dark, I can't even see you right now and you're two inches away from me."

"Sorry, sweetheart."

I reach down and blindly grab for his hand and guide him back to the front walkway to my condo before I stop and turn back to him.

"What are you doing here at this hour?" I ask him, looking up into those blue eyes I constantly find myself getting lost in.

"Would you believe me if I told you I was heading into work?"

Taking a chance, I wrap my arms around his waist and rest my chin on his chest, gazing up at him with the hope that he understands how thrilled I am to see him at this moment. That he was all I could think of during the party tonight.

Cooper follows my lead and slips his arms around my shoulders, bringing me an inch closer to him as he looks back down at me, with something unfamiliar to me in his eyes.

"Not really," I reply, even though it is completely possible that he was headed into work since my condo is on the way.

"What if I told you that I wanted to make sure that my mom decided not to participate in the stupid toy party?"

Laughing, I bury my face in his chest as I shake my head. "Nope."

"What if I told you that I missed you and that I didn't want to go another night without the chance to bury my dick deep inside your hot wet pussy?"

And cue the soaked panties.

Breathlessly I slide one of my hands up his chest, mesmerized at the way his own breath catches at my touch.

"I'd tell you that I may be having the same thoughts."

"What can we do about it?"

At first, I think about the places we could go, and I come up empty. Looking over my shoulder I see his bike and realize that leaves us no option, then I look up at the brown stones before us up toward the second-floor window of my bedroom.

"Can we be quiet?"

He looks at me inquisitively then follows my eyes up to the window before turning back to me with a knowing grin. "The question is, sweetheart, can you keep quiet?"

"Let's find out."

Taking his hands from around my shoulders, he uses one of his thumbs to swipe across my lower lip. My body trembles at the touch and as he leans forward and presses those soft lips against mine, my entire body gives itself over to him.

We lose ourselves into the kiss, into the feeling of being wrapped up in each other, so much so that we don't notice the cars passing until a rowdy group of teens honk their horn as they drive by.

Pulling apart, we gaze at each other with eyes full of hunger and desire. My hands grip at his shirt wanting to pull him just an inch closer.

"Take me upstairs, sweetheart."

Nodding, I release my grip on his shirt, leaving a wrinkled mess in its wake as I reach down to grab his hand and guide him up the set of stairs leading to my front door. I release my keys from the spring bracelet wrapped around my wrist and quietly unlock the deadbolt with Cooper's hot and hard body pressing up against me from behind, his erection pressing into my back as he leaves a trail of kisses along my neck.

It takes a few tries but finally I get the door unlocked and opened to the sound of snoring coming from the living room. Turning toward Cooper, I gesture with a finger over my mouth to be quiet as I tug him across the threshold. A moaning sound comes from the couch as I close the door and I watch in horror as Elle sits up on the couch and looks at Cooper in confusion.

"Cooper?" she asks.

I'm about to speak up, but he beats me to it instead. "Hey, Elle," he whispers. "Why don't you head to bed?"

"Good idea," Elle replies and stumbles from the couch. Luckily Cooper catches her and guides her to the guest bedroom where her kids typically sleep.

I look down at the three other women laying on the floor and loveseat, each with throw pillows under their heads. Reaching into a woven basket that I keep in the corner, I grab a few blankets and cover our friends with them before turning out the pendant light in my kitchen.

Looking into the hallway, I see Cooper leaning against the wall, his large frame taking over most of the space, and my heart jumps in my chest. Never in a million years did I ever think that I would consider changing my ways or changing my thoughts about relationships, but slowly Cooper is causing a shift deep inside me. And I'm both nervous and terrified. But I can't stop. I'm pulled to him in a way that I've never been with anyone. Considering our unusual first meeting, a memory that burned itself into my chest so many years ago, I'm not surprised that once I decided to give my body over to Cooper that I'd begin to question everything. I can't deny the pull, the desire, or the feelings any longer. But that doesn't mean I'm ready to do something about them.

With the crook of his finger, my body follows his command and I amble toward his call in the dark hallway. Wordlessly, we walk toward my bedroom, a place I've been anxious to have him inside.

In the corner, a lamp on my dresser shines, illuminating the room in a soft glow. From behind Cooper I look at my room and try to see it through his eyes. The room is light and airy, mostly white linens with ash colored wood furniture. Not overly girly.

I expect him to say something, anything, but instead, he closes and locks the bedroom door wordlessly and moves to sit on the bed, holding out his hand toward me. I willingly place my hand in his, my body falling under his hypnotizing spell.

With steady hands he grips the edge of my shirt and pulls it over my head, the loose waves of my hair falling and curling around my lace covered breasts. With a jump, I'm tugged forward another step, and I rest my hands on Cooper's shoulders as he presses a soft kiss right above my navel and then works his way across my hip with more soft pecks.

I'm so lost in the nips and licks of his mouth that I barely register when my pants fall to my ankles in a pool of denim. In my haze, I slip off my flats and kick my jeans behind me. Once free from my confines, his rugged hands slide up the back of my thighs and past the barrier of my lace panties to grip my ass in his palms. A rumbling groan vibrates against my stomach as he squeezes my cheeks in his hands.

"Your skin is so soft. I bet you're already wet for me."

Cooper doesn't wait for a response, nor do I think he wants one. He slides his hand under my ass toward the center of my thighs finding me slick with desire for him.

Throwing my head back in pleasure, I moan his name, my voice sounding more like a growl to my own ears.

"What do you want, sweetheart?" he asks as he continues to torment my body with his hand sliding between my folds.

"Your dick," I growl as my hips rock against his hand trying to guide his movements, but the stubborn bastard ignores my pleas.

Slipping a finger inside my channel, I almost sigh with relief, but even with the thrusting of his finger, it's not the sensation I'm seeking.

"More," I groan as I close my eyes and picture myself riding his cock.

He joins another finger deep in my sheath. "This isn't enough for you?" he teases and it's as if the man has a death wish.

My head pops up on my neck, fanning my hair all around my face, and I look down to find Cooper staring up at me with a grin as wide as the Grand Canyon, but I don't miss the tight restraint he's keeping on himself. A restraint holding back his dominant side to take over and fuck me wildly. A restraint that I'm about to break.

"Cooper, I swear that if you don't put your massive cock inside me right now, I'm going to kick you out of this room and make use of one of those toys from earlier."

A flash of something malevolent crosses his face and he slowly retrieves his hand from beneath my panties and stands to his full height. Wordlessly, he strips himself of his shirt, toes off his shoes and socks, and then shimmies himself free of his jeans and boxers, his cock springing against his stomach when it's let loose from behind its barriers.

Cooper has always been larger than me, both in height and muscles, and now as he peers down at me with flames flickering in his eyes I know that I've always underestimated his ability to keep a tight leash on his control. I've poked the bear and now he's awake. . .and hungry.

A strong band wraps around my waist, hoisting me into the air and against his firm body. Then I'm floating, flying through the air to land at the head of the bed. Cooper crawls over the edge of the bed as I bounce and once my body settles he tugs on my ankle to bring me under him.

In the dim light his body gleams, his tanned skin showcasing the intricate black tattoos across his shoulders and arms. If I wasn't a fan of tattoos before, I definitely am now. His arms flex as he reaches a hand under my neck and tilts my head up toward him, bringing my mouth into his reach.

He devours my kiss as if it's the sweetest nectar and he needs it to survive. It heats my body all over, I'm burning for him from just his kiss, and when his hand moves from behind my head to squeeze my breast my blood begins to boil.

The asshole begins to tease my core, sliding his rigid cock against my folds. I pray that he gives into my urges, silently begging that he stops his relentless torment.

Groaning his name as he creeps just the head of his erection into my sex and then withdrawing it, I forcibly reach up and grip his hair as I push at his shoulder with my other hand. I'm surprised when he rolls over on the bed, taking me with him, so that I'm straddling his hips, his large dick standing at attention just under my entrance. Gripping his stiff shaft in my hand, I guide it across my folds, my wetness coating his erection with every pass until I can no longer stand it and I need to have him inside me.

Slowly I lower myself onto his shaft until his entire cock is buried deep inside me, and for a moment, I feel complete. Not just the fullness that I get whenever we come together intimately, but a feeling that all of the shattered pieces of my world have been righted and put back together seamlessly.

"I need you to move," Cooper snarls through gritted teeth as his eyes stare up at me. Eyes that convey how thin the line is tethering him to his self-control.

"Bossy." The corners of my lips tip up in a grin as I rise a few inches and then sink back down onto his erection, slowly, methodically, painstakingly if Cooper's eyes rolling back into his head are any indication.

I trail my fingers up his abdomen, letting my nails scrape against every hill and divot of his stomach until I reach his chest. Flicking his left nipple with my thumb his body jerks beneath me, so I repeat the motion with the right nipple, each deserving the same amount of attention.

With my hands gripping his chest I rock my hips, his cock sliding in and out of my sex with each plunge.

With every slide down his shaft, my clit rubs against the area just above his erection, and it electrifies me. My thrusts become wild and unfettered as I seek my orgasm which is just out of my reach.

I dig my nails into his chest, probably breaking his beautiful skin, but I'm too lost to notice.

"I'm so close," I groan into the dimness of the room, my skin heated as I chase something just out of my reach.

Cooper's sturdy arms reach around my waist and pull me against him. The sweat dripping down my body mingles with his as our chests collide. Soon Cooper fills me with his powerful thrusts as my hips rock back against him.

"Oh, fuck," I say as I squeeze my eyes tightly, the pleasure coming strong and fast. One of the arms wrapped around my waist grips the back of my head, holding me against his body. And when I reach the pinnacle, I do so spectacularly. My body quivers in waves, over and over again. My back arches even under the confines of his hold. And a cry of pleasure pours from my throat, but to keep from waking our neighbors in the other room, I bite down onto Cooper's shoulders to silence my exclamation.

He growls at my intrusion and forcefully pulls my head back to gaze at me. "My turn," he tells me, capturing my mouth with his as he flips us over so that

I'm resting on my back and he's hovering above me. Throughout the entire motion, he stays buried inside me, where he belongs. In my haze, I barely register him reaching across the bed and grabbing a scarf which he rolls up and shoves into my mouth. My eyes immediately narrow at the intrusion.

"Just to keep you quiet, sweetheart. Now, you may want to hold on tight."

Clutching my ankles firmly planted at his hips he brings them up and toward his head to rest them on his shoulders. In the past, this position was always too uncomfortable for me, even though I'm flexible. The guys never seemed to know how to properly position themselves as they jackhammered their hips into me. But I should have known that Cooper would be a different story.

He starts off slowly, rotating his hips in a circle against me allowing me to adjust to the new position. In a measured pace, he drives himself in and out of my channel, and silently I begin to question his need to muffle my screams.

"Fuck, you're gorgeous. If I could look at you like this all of the time, I'd stay buried in you all day. Your pussy is so fucking warm and tight."

Dirty talk, I'm a sucker for it, especially from the sexy man currently feeding his cock into my sex.

A quiver shudders down the walls of my core and Cooper moans in appreciation. In response, he reaches between our bodies and rubs circles around my clit with his thumb causing another wave of pleasure to ripple through me.

"You want more, baby?"

I try to respond, but with the gag in my mouth, all I can do is nod my head, because it's true I want so much more than he's giving me right now.

Leaning forward, Cooper floats above me, and my legs are bent on either side of my chest. The thrusts that had been slow and steady, enough to bring me down from my earlier orgasm, begin to pick up in pace and strength. He slams his hips against me, pushing me forward on the bed only to be stopped by the cushion of my upholstered headboard. He repeats the motion over and over until we're so lost in each other than I barely notice the beads of sweat dripping off of his chest onto me.

"God, I'm so fucking close, sweetheart," Cooper claims as he tosses the scarf from my mouth, grips my jaw and tilts my head upward, then seals our mouths together.

The kiss is feral and rough, our gasps of pleasure mixed with the need to taste each other. My legs drop from his shoulders and he maneuvers his arm between my body and the bed, holding himself close to me.

Cooper pounds his erection into me as he pulls away from my mouth and buries his face into my neck. The powerful grip he holds on my back tightens as he releases himself into me and I realize that I'm going to have a Cooper hand-sized bruise in that spot, which I gladly accept. His body jolts above me in convulsions as he spills himself inside my sex.

We lay like this for a few minutes, our bodies connected by more than just a physical bearing, but something more that has entwined us together.

"Can we stay like this forever?" Cooper asks, his voice heavy, filled with pleasure and lust.

Stroking my hand up and down his muscled back, I consider his words and I wait for the fear to slither its way through me, and I'm surprised when all I feel is contentment.

Unfortunately something more pressing calls to me.

"Maybe we should move first; it's about to get really messy," I tell him and he lifts up to look down at me which causes his softening dick to slide free from me.

"What do you mean?"

"We didn't use a condom, and well, that gets a bit messy."

His eyes widen and I think it's in fear as he rears back onto his heels and stares down at my swollen lips watching as his cum drips from my opening.

"Fuck, that's hot," he whispers, reaching out with a finger and swirling his semen around my pussy.

Sitting up I grip his forearm bringing his attention away from my sex and back to me.

"I'm protected, Cooper."

His movements stop and he looks at me in confusion.

"You're mine, Sara. It wouldn't matter if you weren't."

"I'm not anyone's, Cooper."

He leans toward me, his fascination with my slick pussy now forgotten, and I fall back against the bed.

"I just came inside you and marked you, sweetheart. You're mine," he states, pressing his mouth against mine silencing my argument. His shaft hardens against my hip and my greedy sex clenches in need. Somehow he must know because his sneaky hand slips between my legs again. "You're mine and you like it," he whispers against my lips.

And as I lose myself in him again I realize that he's right, despite my fears, I do like it.

Reaching across the bed with the mid-morning sun streaming through my windows, I find the sheets cool and the bed empty. My body aches all over and as I twist in the bed, I have to fight back the pain from the movement. Looking toward my empty bathroom, I take in the spotless floor where his pants had fallen the night before.

Waking up alone isn't unfamiliar to me. Usually I'm the one leaving before the sun rises, but today the loneliness feels different somehow.

With measured steps, I slowly make my way to the shower and let the warm water wash away some of the aches and pains left by the man that masterfully took my body to new heights more times than I can count.

Dressed and with a pile of laundry in my arms, I head down the hall, and I'm surprised to find Elle sitting at my kitchen counter with a steaming cup of coffee in her hand.

"Good morning, sunshine," I greet her and look into the living room to find the pillows and blankets from last night that I had given our other guests have been neatly placed back on the chairs and in the basket.

"Good morning to you," Elle says in return as she takes a sip of her coffee. "I made you a cup as well when I heard the shower turn on."

Closing the lid on the washer, I start the cycle and then head toward the kitchen for a cup of energy.

"Thanks. Are you feeling okay?"

"Nothing a little ibuprofen can't fix."

Nodding I join her by taking a sip of coffee, but her penetrating gaze lingers on me longer than normal.

Setting my mug on the counter, I cock my head in confusion. "What? Is there something on my face?"

"No, you just look. . .different. . .happy."

"Do I not normally look happy?"

"No, you usually look like you want to tear the world a new one."

"Oh."

"It couldn't happen to have anything to do with a certain someone that helped me to my bed last night, could it?" Elle inquires as she steeples her fingers in front of her face inquisitively.

I can feel my cheeks begin to blush, so I attempt to hide them by taking another sip of my coffee. "What makes you say that?"

"I've been waiting for you two to bring your heads out of the sand, but you're both stuck in your own ways. Wishful thinking I suppose."

"Nothing is going on with Cooper and me," I lie. "He stopped by on his way to work because I told him that I needed help getting you to bed, you lush."

"Mmhmm."

"Elle, you know how I feel about relationships."

"People change," she quips and then leans over the counter to place her now empty mug in my sink. "Want to do something fun today?"

"Maybe, I have a stack of laundry a mile high and it's my first weekend without wedding duty."

"Well, add one more item to that wedding list."

"Ugh," I groan at the thought of losing another weekend. "What now?"

"I need to go buy a wedding dress and I want my best friend with me."

Elation soars through me and I hastily swallow all of my coffee, ignoring the burn as it travels down my throat. I rush around the corner and kiss Elle's cheek as I head back toward my bedroom to change.

"This is the day I have been waiting for!" I shout into my empty room, Cooper's absence long forgotten.

Opening my closet door, I slip on a sundress and a pair of sandals before scurrying into the bathroom to swipe on a layer of mascara. Just as I rush from my bedroom, I notice Elle propped on the bar stool in her cut off shorts and tank top from yesterday. That won't do. I grab another sundress from my closet, one that is a bit too small for me, and I toss it to Elle as I pass her to grab my car keys.

At this point, she knows not to argue with me and she heads toward the guest room to change. To kill time I take a seat on my couch and flip through a home décor magazine before my eyes settle on the decorative bowl I have resting in the center. A bowl that holds an origami heart.

Cooper.

I rest the delicate masterpiece in the palm of my hand, admiring the detailed folds when it flips against my fingers revealing the opposite side that says, "Open." Meticulously I unfold the small treasure to expose the handwritten note from Cooper.

You're Beautiful and Mine.

I read it over one, two, three times, memorizing each swoosh of his handwritten scroll. If this is how the man plans to win me over, he's definitely getting off to a great start.

The sound of water rushes to my ears and I slip down the hall as Elle brushes her teeth in my guest bath, not wanting her to find the note from Cooper and inflame more questions. I tuck the note away in my nightstand so that I can admire it later and make my way back out to the hall at the same time as Elle.

"Ready, future Mrs. Divers?" I ask her, noting the warmth on her pale cheeks. As she nods, we walk together out toward my car and I have to keep myself from looking toward the alleyway where Cooper had snuck up on me last night.

"You, okay?" Elle asks as she notices my distraction and I realize that I've walked past my car that she is standing beside.

"Yeah, sorry. I'm in my own world. Now, come on. Let's go find you the most beautiful gown for my beautiful best friend."

Chapter Twelve

Cooper

MY OFFICE IS THE last place that I want to be on a Sunday afternoon, especially since I had just left Sara's place this morning, but when my partner called saying that an owner of a local business has started receiving threats, I came in to figure things out.

A few patrol officers stroll past my open door and thank me for the box of coffee cake that I stole out of Jackson and Elle's fridge this morning. I made sure to leave a note, but she's going to kill me anyway. Elle doesn't take too kindly to me stealing her baked goods.

Rummaging through the file that José, my partner, left on my desk I make a few notes next to some key people of interest related to the person receiving the threats. It's not until I skim down to the bottom that I notice he and his wife are going through a bitter divorce, one that is going to split up their shares of the business. And the name listed on the file has been marked through with a red pen and renamed Sara Campbell.

Of course, the woman throwing my world for a spin is tied up in this nasty divorce that is about to get worse when I have to start questioning all of the family regarding the death threats the husband has received. Luckily, the person sending the threatening voicemail happened to be a male, so that leaves her out, for the most part. It's not uncommon to hire people.

Dropping the paper from my grasp, I bury my hands in my hair. "Shit."

"Hey, man," José calls out as he takes a seat at his desk in the corner of our office. "What's up?"

"Have you read through this file yet?"

"Naw, I figured you'd tell me all about it."

"José," I groan as I hold the file out for him to take and review. "Read it and tell me if you see anything interesting."

Begrudgingly he stands and grabs the folder from me before going back to his seat. I watch as his eyes skim the paper and I can tell immediately when he reaches Sara's name. It's not common for us to red pen an area in our initial investigation, especially when I know that the attorney marked off is one from her office.

"Isn't this?"

"The woman I've been spending time with? Yeah, it is."

José looks at me and then drops the file on his desk while leaning back in his chair, his muscled arms tucked behind his head.

"You like her."

My cold stare only causes him to laugh more. "It doesn't matter if I like her, she's my brother's fiancée's best friend. I wish she weren't tied up in this."

"Well, it's a little too late for wishing now. If you want, I can be the one to question her if it comes to it, which I doubt that it will."

"Yeah, I appreciate that. Fingers crossed that we figure out the threats before it comes to that."

In our town, there isn't a large amount of crime that requires a lot of immediate attention, but we are located on the outskirts of Greenville, South Carolina and occasionally some of the ruckus spills our way. Summer is already making headway and we've only had two homicides in our area thus far.

Scribbling away some notes from some domestic battery cases we worked on earlier in the week, I hear a knock on my desk and look up to find José with his backpack draped over his shoulder. I take note of the darkness bleeding through the blinds and realize that I've worked through dinner.

He gestures his goodbye and we agree to meet for breakfast before working tomorrow. I follow suit and pack up my belongings, but as my eye catches the file with Sara's name once more, I hesitate before leaving it on top of the remainder of my files and shoving my laptop into my bag.

Whipping out my phone, I shoot a text to Sara asking if I can stop by and she quickly responds in agreement. With a smile on my face, I pick up a bit of food and make my way to her apartment like it's second nature. And with the way that she greets me when she opens the door, it must seem like second nature to her as well. Her legs wrap around my waist and she plunges her tongue deep inside my mouth. My take-out is long forgotten as I carry her back to the bedroom and decide to spend my night lost in this woman determined to drive me crazy.

My phone buzzes on the nightstand in Sara's room and I moan as I twist my tired body away from the warmth of Sara pressed up against me. We never laid down any rules regarding spending the night after sex, it just sort of flowed into that category and I'm not complaining.

"Hey." I yawn as I answer Maureen's call, the dispatch for the night. She tells me that there have been some developments in a recent case and the Chief wants me and José to scrutinize them as soon as possible.

"Alright, I'll be in shortly."

Ending the call, I turn back over and pull Sara toward me.

"Mmm, was that work?" she mumbles in a sleep filled voice against my chest, her delicate fingers tracing one of my tattoos across my chest.

"Yeah, I need to go in."

She nods as she brushes her lips against my chest, her kiss sending a current directly to my cock. Needing to look into her captivating eyes, I run one hand through her hair and tilt her head back as I capture her kiss with my own. Our tongues brush and I watch in fascination as she fully comes awake and she rocks her body against me.

Her hand slips between our bodies and she wraps her palm and fingers around my achingly hard shaft causing it to jerk in her hold.

"Do you have time for this?" she asks in between kisses.

And of course, I answer by pulling away from her kiss and sucking one of her pert nipples into my mouth as I slide my cock inside her tight box until I'm buried to the hilt.

With a pop, I pull away from her breast as I tell her, "I always have time for this."

An hour later I'm strolling into the office with a hot cup of coffee and a smile that actually hurts my cheeks, but I can't turn it off. Waking up buried deep inside Sara is something that I need to plan on a daily basis. My appearance is the complete opposite of José who sits in a shirt half-untucked from his pants and his hair askew. He's munching on a donut probably not even realizing that he has jelly hanging from his chin.

"Hey, is the Chief in?" I ask as I sit my bag on my desk, glad that I keep a few spare clothes inside just in case I'm out when I get a call.

"Yeah, he came in about the same time as me. What has you so bright eyed and bushy tailed this morning?

My grin grows wider and the bastard shakes his head in jealousy.

"Man, you got fucking laid. Wishing I was you right now. All I got was a stripper teasing me. To be one of the lucky ones," he muses as he wipes his chin clean with a tissue then walks toward the door.

Grabbing my notebook and the files from yesterday, I follow José to Chief Sanderson's office. He briefs us on some new developments in the case regarding Mr. Cullan's death threats and how a faulty bomb was found in a box delivered to his house. But also how the same box was delivered to the residence where Mrs. Cullan is currently staying.

"So, it's not the wife or the husband. Is there anyone else we should be looking into?" José asks as I open the file and read through the suspect list and details.

"I want to question the older children. They're all in their twenties and, my guess is that they're looking at a hefty payout if the parents are out of the picture."

"And still married," José tacks on and I nod in agreement.

The Chief advises us to contact them first, get their alibi, and then report back as he has the on-call detective collecting the evidence for us. José piles into the passenger seat of my unmarked car and we head to the eldest's home to find he has already left for work, and as we arrive at his office at the Cullan's headquarters he's at a meeting and unavailable.

Luckily, the daughter works in the accounting department at the same location and we're able to track her down and proceed with a few questions. The way the young woman visibly shakes as we ask about any odd packages being delivered, I can tell that she isn't hiding anything. But until we can go through the evidence more thoroughly, we can't definitively rule her out.

"Come on, I think we need to get a bit more information about the son. It seems like he's steering clear of us on purpose," I point out just as my cell phone rings in my pocket.

I surprised to see Elle's name flash across the screen.

"Hey, Elle. What's up?" I say, just as José goes through our calls missed while we were interviewing. "Hey, man. You need to hear this."

"Hold on, Elle," I tell her but she keeps babbling on the phone as I cover the receiver. "What's going on, José?"

"There has been a fire at your girl's work. I'm sorry, man."

My chest begins to beat wildly and the sweat pooling on my palms threatens to slip my phone free as I shakingly bring it to my ear.

"Elle?" I whisper, praying that she isn't calling with bad news.

"You need to get to the hospital. Sara got hurt during the explosion."

I end the call without waiting to hear more. I just know that my heart is resting on a lumpy bed somewhere hurt and scared.

"Fuck, Sara's hurt. I need to go."

"I understand. The building is on the way, drop me off and I'll see what I can find out. Go to your lady."

Silently we speed down the highway until I turn off to head downtown. José jumps from the car before I even make a complete stop, but at that moment the heat from the flames sears my skin through the crack in the door. As much as I want to stay and figure out what happened, I have a more pressing place to be – by my girl's side.

I hate the hospital. It's too bright. It smells like a weird combination of life, death, and bleach. And it's an endless corridor of unanswered questions. Like, why won't anyone let me back to see my woman?

"She's having X-rays completed, sir. When she's brought back to her room, I will let you know when you can go back to see your fiancée."

"Fine," I grunt as I stomp my way to a seat giving me a prime view of the double doors leading to her room. I'm not even aware of what floor I'm on, I just followed the guidance of a petite older woman who took pity on me when I arrived frantically asking to see Sara. I'm not aware when an arm wraps around my shoulders or when a small head rests on my bicep.

"How long have you been waiting?" Jackson asks.

"Too fucking long."

I hear him mumble his understanding, but I never pull my attention away from those damn double doors that mock me every time that they open.

"Want to tell us why you're here giving every doctor that walks through those doors a death glare?"

"No," I growl, and even though I don't turn to face him, I can hear the smile on his face when he says, "About time."

"Oh, that's Sara's mom." Elle points toward the well-dressed woman that breezes through the lobby entrance with a burly man trailing behind her. I know that I've met her on occasion, but never to the point where I'd feel the need to analyze our meeting. Now I wish that I had.

The woman looks like a smaller version of her daughter, with a smartly cut hairdo framing her face. The blonde locks curving right under her chin showcase the elegant pearls draped around her neck. The man she's with is her complete opposite, looking more like the Brawny man than a high society figure.

At the reception desk, the nurse points in our direction and Sara's mom rushes toward Elle and envelopes her in a tight embrace. She asks us if we've heard anything and everyone stares down at me in question, but all I can do is shake my head and keep my stare locked on the door. If I focus on the people coming in and out of the area, then my mind doesn't have a chance to wander toward the what ifs. What if she's hurt? What if she's in critical condition? What if she's dead?

The last question has me taking a staggering breath and I finally pull my gaze away to look down at the floor between my feet.

A small hand rests against my upper back and the touch is warm, kind. "My girl is a fighter, don't you worry."

For the first time since I've arrived, I turn to gaze at the woman with eyes that see far more than they should, and they are filled with a knowing gleam.

"I. . uh," I begin but luckily we're interrupted by the doctor as she calls for the family of Sara Campbell. I rise immediately, Sara's mother's hand falling from my back.

"Are you the fiancé?" she asks, and Jackson coughs from behind me while Elle stifles a giggle.

"Yes, how is she? Can I see her?"

"I can take one back there at a time, considering the circumstances," she explains, and my stomach drops as I begin to imagine the worst-case scenario.

Turning to look at her mother I find her gripping Elle's hand, both women with tears sprinkling the edges of their lashes.

"One of you should go back to be with her," I tell them and Elle looks as if she's ready to jump at the chance to be with her best friend, but Sara's mother holds back and shakes her head. "No, she will want to see you first. Just make sure she knows that we're waiting."

Sullenly I follow the doctor through the double doors that I had hoped would be my salvation, but instead, seem like my demise. As we round the corner, I hear some commotion coming from a room just as a nurse rushes into the hall. I look at the doctor questionably, but she just shakes her head.

I expect us to continue walking, but the doctor leaves me in front of the room I had been watching and takes a step inside. Following her lead, I take in the boring appearance of the room until my eyes settle on a vision wrapped in gauze and covered in soot.

"Can I leave now?" Sara asks the doctor as she touches the dressing wrapped around her head with a hand enfolded in a bandage. Seeing her alive, awake, and mostly intact I breathe a sigh of relief and have to lean forward feeling as my adrenaline crashes. "Cooper? What are you doing here?"

Before I can answer, the doctor assures us that she is preparing the discharge papers now, something Sara claims she has been insisting on since she arrived by the urgency of the paramedics. The doctor explains that they needed to X-ray her wrist to verify that it wasn't broken before they could discharge her.

My guess is that Sara has been a problem patient, but my relief must be palpable in the room because as the doctor turns to exit, she smiles and pats my back assuring me that my fiancée will be okay in a few weeks.

"Fiancée?" Sara asks as she sits on the edge of the bed.

"How else was I going to get back here?"

"Touché," she says, and I notice her bottom lip quiver. It's a glimpse of Sara that she's never shown, a vulnerability that she keeps tightly sealed behind her walls of brick and mortar.

I take a seat beside her on the bed and wrap her in my arms, and luckily she buries her head against my chest, giving me a moment to savor the feel of her in my arms. Something I was fearful may never happen against as every deadly scenario possible had traveled through my mind while I sat in the waiting room.

"Tell me what happened," I urge.

"It was awful. I was sitting in my office getting ready for a meeting with my client and then I heard a group of people arguing in the hall, which was strange enough because everyone else was scheduled for a staff meeting. The shouting was getting so loud that I could barely think, so I stuck my head out in the hall to confront them, but when I looked in their direction, everyone started running.

"I didn't have time to react. I slammed my office door shut and threw an office chair through the window just as the explosion happened. I landed on the ground outside my office and then took off running. I'm lucky I got out with a sprained wrist and a few stitches. From what I've learned everyone else has burns over most of their body and broken limbs."

My heart breaks for her because even though she's in pain, I know that she reached out to the hospital staff to make sure the rest of the employees survived.

"Sweetheart, do you know who may have done this?"

"Yeah. See I had a meeting scheduled, and when the yelling started, I noticed it was Mr. Nemmer, Ms. Cullan, and her son. They were all arguing because Ms. Cullan has been having an affair with Mr. Nemmer, which is why I had to take over the case. My guess is the son found out."

Unfortunately, I now have the main suspect for the threats against Mr. and Ms. Cullan. It's just a travesty that Sara and her coworkers have got themselves wrapped up in it.

"I'm really glad you're here, Cooper."

I turn on the bed to face her and gently place my hands on her cheeks, careful to mind her stitches. "When I got the news I rushed right over. I've been pacing a hole in the floor as I waited for any news. I'm so glad to see with my own eyes that you're okay. Don't scare me like that again. I don't think my heart can stand it."

I don't expect a reply, knowing that Sara is still working through this influx of feelings for me that I know have suddenly crashed upon her.

My thumb moves across her cheek to swipe against her plump lip and her sneaky tongue peaks out to taste the tip of my finger. "You don't have to say anything, sweetheart. As I told you before, I'm not going anywhere."

But I won't lie, it does sting to know that I've practically told her that I'm in love with her and she can't return the emotion. But I know that I'm not wasting my time. Sara can feel and love, she just has to allow herself to do so.

A nurse knocks on the door with a wheelchair waiting in the hall.

"Are you here to bust me out?" Sara gleefully asks the young woman with a few papers in her hand.

"Yes, I am. I just need to you sign these and then we'll be on our way."

I follow them out of the hospital, Sara's mom and Elle joining the group until we reach the entrance. I offer to take Sara home and everyone agrees. I just don't tell them that I'm taking her to my home, where she should be.

She settles in my car and I assure her mother that I'll make sure that she takes it easy. Of course, my idiot brother mumbles under his breath that I will be making sure that I pay extra attention to Sara. Bastard.

"My condo is in the other direction," she points out as I turn out of the hospital.

"I'm taking you to my place so I can make sure that you rest."

"Cooper, I. . ."

Reaching out I move my hand from the gear shift on the console between our seats and rest it on her thigh.

When we brake at the stoplight, I turn to face Sara. "I thought I lost you today. Please just humor me and let me take care of you."

Her face softens, and for a short moment, I feel as if I've won the battle.

"Just temporary, Cooper. It's just until I'm healed up."

"Sure, sweetheart," I lie. "Whatever you say."

Luckily Sara drops the argument and by the time we pull up to my house behind Elle and Jackson she's passed out in the passenger seat. I carry her limp body into my house and head straight for the bedroom where I gently lay her on the bed. She immediately curls into herself, wincing as her stitches pull against the pillow.

"Sleep well, sweetheart," I tell her as I exit the room and close the door.

In my home office, I log into my email and shoot a message to Jose and the Chief disclosing the situation Sara described. If my hunches are right then the Cullan's oldest son is about to find himself neck deep in trouble and my fist, because no one is going to hurt my girl.

Chapter Thirteen

Sara

IT'S BEEN A WEEK since I moved back to my home against Cooper's will. He was hurt and it was painful to leave the comfort of his bed and his waiting on me hand and foot, but I was getting overwhelmed. The fears that kept me from relationships all those years ago started creeping in whenever we were together. The fear of losing myself. The fear of being chained to a person that could destroy my world. And with Cooper's job, the fear of my heart being ripped out, if not by him, if by some outside force. Something I couldn't control. And perhaps that is the crux of my fear, the lack of control over something that can change my life.

And after watching my mother hop from husband to husband, and watching her complete devastation after each marriage ended, I know what I'm in store for.

My phone buzzes on the coffee table and I glance down to see Cooper's name flash on the screen. I've been actively ignoring him even though my chest aches every time that I do so. I'm not even sure what the messages say, I've been letting them queue up instead.

But today I can no longer ignore him, it's one of our last meetings with Kerry and Taylor. I considered backing out, claiming that I'm still trying to get my work together since the explosion.

The explosion that left our clients scrambling for new representation and me seriously considering moving to a new firm. The Cullan's son was convicted on attempted murder and multiple other charges toward his parents.

Checking the clock on the wall, I realize that I'm running late, so I grab my keys and head out of the apartment that feels far less like home than Cooper's house.

Taking the steps toward my car, I don't notice the motorcycle double parked beside my vehicle or the sexy man standing against my driver's side door with his arms crossed against his chest.

"Cooper," I whisper in surprise, and the man just shakes his head sullenly.

Taking a step toward me, he asks, "Are you done ignoring me?"

"I wasn't ignoring you," I tell him as I try to sidestep but he just follows me.

"Could have fooled me."

Rolling my eyes as I finally step around his body he reaches out and grabs my wrist. The movement is quick and fierce, but gentle at the same time.

"We need to talk, Sara. When I said you were mine, I meant it. I thought we were moving in a new direction after the accident."

I don't want to tell him that he's right, I was, but then my head got the better of me. And being a wishy-washy person is so far from my normal personality. I needed to come home to return to a neutral territory.

Instead, I ignore him. "Let me go, Cooper."

He releases my wrist and steps over to his bike, and I believe that the argument is over, but just as I open my door, he adds, "I'll see you there, Sara. But this isn't over, not by a long shot." Then before I can reply he hops on his bike and revs the engine.

Great.

I arrive at the steakhouse Kerry had suggested, the same restaurant where I had laid eyes on Cooper over a year ago. Funny that this is the place that could serve as the beginning and end for us.

He's already seated at the table with the event planning team when I arrive. The women greet me warmly with smiles and hugs. Cooper doesn't look up from his stare on the menu which causes Kerry to look between us in confusion. But the woman minds her business and gestures for me to take a seat, unsurprisingly beside Cooper.

He continues to ignore me as Kerry brings out her checklist and begins to discuss all of the items we've covered, but as she delves into some of the ceremony decorations that we need to finalize today a strong hand reaches out and grips onto my thigh. And it's as if my world changes from black and white into a world of color just at his touch.

Embers sizzle beneath the surface of my skin at his touch and I barely register the words Kerry says and the pictures Taylor holds out. I'm not even sure what I'm agreeing to, but hopefully, Kerry doesn't notice how out of sorts I seem.

When the waiter comes by to take our lunch order, I haven't even had a chance to peruse the menu, and with the way my stomach is flip-flopping, I'm not sure I can eat much anyway. But before I have the chance to tell the server that I'm not eating, Cooper orders me a small salad and a bowl of soup.

I sneer as I turn to face him, but the frustrating man just shrugs his shoulders. "You need to eat," he says.

Opening my mouth to tell him how I feel about him ordering for me, I'm interrupted when Kerry asks if Elle and Jackson have mentioned any plans for their honeymoon.

"They are planning a trip to Walt Disney World with the kids a few days after the wedding."

With a curious expression, Kerry takes a sip of her wine and then pulls out a business card. "I always believe that a couple needs a little alone time following their wedding. This is the number for a new bed and breakfast about an hour and a half from here. You two should go check it out, the town has a lot to do and I think it would be a great little vacation for them. And if you think that it will work, I'm sure we can negotiate a stay for them and someone to watch the kids."

I try to mask the shake of my hand as I reach for the business card, but I fail miserably.

"Are you okay?" Kerry asks, and I try to smile and nod.

"Just low blood sugar I guess."

"Well, it's a good thing Cooper ordered you some food."

Luckily our food arrives not much later and the group silences as we enjoy our meals. I'll never let Cooper know how delicious the soup is once it settles in my stomach. He still hasn't removed his hand from my leg through the entire lunch and I'm surprised our party hasn't noticed since he is eating his steak one-handed, a feat I'm impressed by to say the least.

"Okay, so please take a look at the bed and breakfast's website. I think you'll be pleasantly surprised. And I happen to know the owner so we can negotiate a great rate for them for a short stay. It will also give them a nice little reprieve away from the world. Hopefully, you can go by for the weekend and, I know, Sara, you said that you're sort of out of work right now so this may be the perfect opportunity."

"Well, I'm still working with a few clients from my home office, but I'm sure we can make a day trip and check it out. That area is known for its wineries, so maybe I can pick up a few suggestions for the reception."

Kerry's face transforms into one of elation as she pulls out her tablet and marks something down. "That is a great idea. I didn't even consider hitting up those wineries for their stock. I'll have to give them a call."

Taylor pipes in reminding Kerry that they have another meeting across town and the women quickly pack up their things in preparation to leave.

Kerry shakes our hands and says, "I'm so glad that I've had the chance to work with you both. From here on out I'll mostly be in contact with Elle until the big day. And hopefully, I'll be planning your weddings one day."

I want to say more, I want to explain that she won't be planning my wedding, but most likely Cooper's. My heart plummets deep into my stomach at the thought of Cooper marrying anyone else, just like I feared. That stubborn heart with pieces sewn and bandaged together. But he deserves someone else. He deserves a beautiful woman that can be with him one hundred percent. I wish so badly that I could be that woman.

She leaves the table with a wave, stranding me alone with Cooper and with a racing heart that I'm certain he can feel beating madly through the fabric of my pants. The tension between us becomes too much to bear as he continues to silently eat his steak with a one-handed elegance that I wish I could master. Mustering up some hidden strength I pull away from his grasp and slip over to the other side of the booth. Cooper drops his fork on his plate with a clatter and stares at me, almost in disbelief.

"Am I that repulsive to you now?" he snarls at me, and I realize that I've actually hurt his feelings by slipping away from him.

"No, I-"

"Look, I get that I may come on strong and that it may seem like I'm trying to wield your hand, but that couldn't be farther from the truth. I'm following your lead, but it seems as if we take two steps forward then you take a giant leap back. Why, Sara? At this point do you really think this is a game? That I'm not in it for the long haul? Hell, at this point I've been imagining a little girl with your blonde hair and blue eyes since our night together a few weeks back. Does it seem like I'm not ready? Tell me what I have to do," he says exasperatedly, his fist pounding on the table in significance causing our water glasses to rattle and the groups beside us to look over in curiosity.

"I don't know what to say, Cooper."

"Of course you don't. You're going to hide behind your parents failed marriage and the failed marriages of your clients as an excuse. I should have figured it out by now." He tosses a few bills on the table, but I can't make out the amount through the moisture pooling in my eyes. He knows my secrets, he knows my shame, he knows the façade I try to hide behind. "Let me know when you go to Carson. I'll meet you there."

"Cooper. . ." I start, but he's already scurrying past the tables and out the door, leaving me to wonder at what point during the lunch things went so horribly wrong. But I know it wasn't lunch, there wasn't any one moment where things went wrong. It was that I never truly allowed things to go right. I kept him at a distance, just close enough to feel that love and affection that I craved, but far enough away to keep from feeling the hurt when things would end. Because they would end, they always did. But then why does it hurt so bad to see him walk away, to see him fed up with my half-assed attempt at an emotionless relationship?

Pulling out my phone I blink away the tears as I hit Elle's number on my favorites.

"Sara?" she asks, probably confused as to why I'd call her, I'm more of a texting person.

Stuttering through my words, I tell her that I think I've messed up. I don't tell her why, or how, but Elle being the friend that she is doesn't need details. Though I'm sure that she is going to require a night of drinking and snacks so that I can fill her in. No, my best friend just offers a simple piece of advice. "Well, if you know you've screwed up, fix it. I don't need to tell you how, you'll figure that out on your own, but you can make things right."

She has no clue that I'm referring to things with Cooper, but I wonder if instinctively she is putting two and two together after the incident in the hospital. Elle's been waiting for her chance to grill me about him, I've been making myself scarce since then.

"You're smart, Sara. Let me know when you're coming over to tell me everything. And I do mean *everything*."

"Thanks, Elle," I whisper as I end the call. It would have been nice to have her tell me exactly what to do, like go buy him tickets to his favorite team (which I never cared to learn) or a bottle of his favorite whiskey (another item I need to add to my growing list), but she knows that I wouldn't listen anyway. I've always been my own person and when someone tells me to do something, I usually do the opposite.

The business card resting on the table catches my eye, and I reach to grab it, holding it out in front of me. That's when an idea strikes me, and my frown flips into a growing smile.

"So, tell me again what happened?" Elle asks from her perch on the couch where she is combing through Kennedy's wet hair as her daughter sits nestled between her legs. Jackson is out in their backyard tossing a ball with Noah and Cooper.

"We've been," I begin as I eye Kennedy in her lap. "Doing things since you forced us to spend time together."

"Unh huh, then what happened?" she inquires as she slips pieces of Kennedy's hair between her fingers to create a braid.

"Then things got complicated. I got scared and pushed him away after he spent time taking care of me at his house."

"Right, right," she nods absentmindedly.

"And now he's pushed me away because he realized that I'm not worth the trouble."

Elle's head whips around at my statement and she looks at me like I've grown two heads.

"Don't, Elle," I tell her, holding my hand up with my palm facing her. "I know I've messed up so I booked us a night at the bed and breakfast I was telling you about."

"Which is really sweet of Kerry to suggest. It will be nice for Jackson and me to get away for a little while. . .alone." Elle finishes up Kennedy's hair and then instructs the preschooler to play with a puzzle on the kitchen table. "Now, back to you. How do you plan to get him to stay?"

"I haven't figured that part out yet, but I'm not above slathering myself in chocolate syrup and presenting myself as his dessert. I'll do whatever it takes."

"Well, I advise against the chocolate, it gets very messy. How about you just tell him how you feel?"

"Because I don't know how I feel! I'm scared out of my fucking-," I shut my mouth quickly when Elle cuts her eyes at me, and I look over at Kennedy who doesn't seem to have heard my mess up. "Freaking mind. You know what I see every day, Elle. Heck, you were one of those relationships that I watched crumble before me. Think about what could have happened to your kids if I hadn't had the brains to get that piece taken care of right away."

"You're right. I absolutely can't imagine the things that you see and hear at work. But, Sara, those people aren't you. Those men aren't Cooper. And I know you use your parent's divorce as a crutch, but look at your mom. Even after all these years, she's still searching for love.

"You can make things work if you try. It's not easy to open yourself up to someone, to make yourself vulnerable, but it's also the best feeling in the world. Just knowing that someone is there for you no matter what; through any sort of circumstance is the best thing in the world.

"I can't promise that things will work out with you and Cooper, but if you try, and let him know that you're willing to try he may come around. Or you can stay in a fancy B&B and have hot monkey sex. I think he'd be up for that regardless of where you guys stand."

"What makes you say that?" I ask her curiously. Maybe she knows something about Cooper that I don't.

"Uh, he's a guy, and you're a smokin' hot female. He'd be dumb to turn you down for sex."

The sliding glass doors leading to her backyard slide open and Noah comes rushing into the kitchen and toward the hallway at break-neck speed, while Jackson casually walks in behind him.

"I guess I'll get out of your hair. Wish me luck," I mumble to Elle as I wrap her in a hug and then wave over to Jackson as I walk out of their house.

By instinct I turn to look over at Cooper's house as I open my car door, admiring the wooden shutters against the whitewashed brick exterior. I miss it. Not just the house, but having a place that felt like home.

My mother and I hopped from apartment to apartment when I was growing up, and my situation right now isn't much different. A condo is just an apartment that I own. But Cooper's house always felt as if it wrapped its arms around me and held me tight.

As if he could feel my stare, I watch as the living room light flicks on and Cooper gazes at me through his window. Our eyes lock, and I inhale a quick breath. He's just as gorgeous as I remember, not that I thought he would change in the three days since I last saw him, but he looks better than my memories serve me. I realized after our lunch last weekend that I didn't even have a photo of him saved on my phone, all I had were stupid memories.

Lost in my thoughts, I startle when he flicks the lights off and turns away from the window, leaving me in the darkness of the night. A darkness that feels all too familiar.

Painstakingly I pull out of the driveway and head back toward my place, and that's when an idea hits me.

Something to capture his attention and at least give me the chance to make things right. Glancing at the clock on the dashboard, I realize that I don't have a lot of time to make it happen, but if there is one thing about me that is tried and true, it's that I'm very determined.

Chapter Fourteen

Cooper

MY HAIR WHIPS AROUND my forehead as I travel down the road with the window down. I run my hand through the overly long strands and know that I can't put off that haircut any longer. I had kept putting it off because I loved the feeling of Sara running her fingers through the strands, especially when she gripped them tight in her fist as she came.

Fuck, just remembering how reckless she was in my arms when she let her guard down has my cock pressing against the zipper of my pants. Which is quite uncomfortable as I drive since I can't really adjust myself.

I chant to myself to think about the way the eldest Cullan son had tried to come onto myself and José yesterday to try to get out of charges. The man was willing to do anything, and I do mean *anything*, to get out of going to prison.

I shiver and my erection immediately shrivels away remembering how the man licked his lips at me. I'm not against same-sex love, but it's just not for me personally.

I pass a sign for Carson, North Carolina on the highway and prepare myself to pull off at the next exit.

Sara never called to ask if I would ride with her, not that I would have. Things with her have exploded into a realm I'm unable to navigate. I know that I said I would give her time, and I am, but recently it felt more like I was being dragged along. And the worst part is that I know I'm in love with her. It wasn't a slow-burning love that happens for most people. It was a smack me in the face as I looked at her one day and I knew that I couldn't be without her. She was it for me. If only she felt the same. It's the reason why I let her go – or so she thinks.

I had gone to my dad for advice after Sara had moved out of my house while I was away at work. He and my mom have been together forever, so he seemed like a logical choice to ask for guidance. But what did the old man say? The age-old saying "If you love her, let her go. If she doesn't come back, then it wasn't meant to be." What he didn't tell me was how much it pained me to tear her apart the way that I did.

Sure, I could have stuck it out for the phenomenal sex and pray that hopefully, she'd come around, but now that I knew without a doubt I was in love with her I wanted more.

Today is going to be hard, seeing her in a beautifully restored home where my brother and his fiancée are going to spend their first few nights as a married couple, a place that I wish I could spend a few nights with Sara. But I have to play this right. I need to make it seem as if being near her isn't tearing me apart inside. She had mentioned only staying in the town for a few hours and then heading back home, but maybe I can convince her to stay for dinner before driving back.

My phone pings with directions as the exit for the town comes into view and it directs me to almost twenty miles of a straight road without much on either side.

Talk about being in the middle of nowhere.

I had plugged in the address of the bed and breakfast after having to call Kerry to retrieve it and it seems to be settled at the edge of the small town. As I drive down Main Street, I take in the front façades of the buildings and the large Victorian homes. It looks like I've been teleported and dropped into a quaint 1950's era town.

I pass a bar called Horizon's, a store called Cassidy's, and a movie theater. A young cop waves from his patrol car as he passes and I mimic the gesture with a confused smile. People call out greetings to others on the sidewalk as they pass, it seems like everyone knows someone in the town.

The next block is filled with more shops, a bakery and grill, and another bar that looks like it's beginning some renovations. The central downtown ends and the road takes a slight curve leading up to a large diner called Angie's that fills my car with some amazing scents as I drive past. A huge building of glass and stone catches me off guard as I continue down the road, noticing a walkway to the pharmacy at the edge of the downtown.

What kind of town is this? I ask myself as I swear I see the lead singer of the rock band Exoneration walking out of the glass building holding the hand of a small woman with black framed glasses perched on her nose.

Shaking my head to free myself of these crazy thoughts I continue down the road, noting that my next turn should be coming up. I slow down the car until I notice a dirt path on the left and make the turn.

I follow for a few hundred yards until I pull up to a Victorian mansion that looks to have been recently restored. A car sits in a small parking area and I recognize it as Sara's along with two others.

Just as I park in between the two unfamiliar cars a couple steps out of the front door, the man's arm wrapped tightly around the woman's shoulders. I'd say they are probably in their late fifties, maybe sixties, but it's obvious that the couple takes good care of themselves.

"Hi," I greet them with a wave as I step across the path toward the covered porch.

"Welcome, I'm Andrea and this is Jack," the woman says in greeting. "You must be Cooper. We're so excited to have you staying with us."

"Oh, I'm not staying. I just came to check out the place for my brother and his fiancée," I explain and the woman looks up at the man, I assume he is her husband if their matching wedding bands are any indication, in confusion.

"Well, then," the man starts. "We have some drinks and baked goods from the local bakery available in the dining area. Please help yourself and then we can give you a tour of the place."

My stomach grumbles at the thought of food and I chuckle in embarrassment. "Food sounds good."

I'm impressed as I walk through the large wooden door and enter a spacious foyer painted a rich maroon color showcasing the restored wooden trim and crown molding. They lead me into a dining room covered in gold wallpaper with an intricate design woven throughout, but my eyes immediately fall onto the smorgasbord of baked concoctions spread on the table.

Grabbing two chocolate chip cookies, I shove one entirely in my mouth and it's quickly followed by the other. I spot a dispenser of water in the corner and I go over to fill a cup.

"We offer scenic winery tours if you and your friend are interested," the woman that introduced herself as Andrea explains. Which has me wondering where Sara is off to.

"Do you happen to know where my friend may be?"

"Oh, she's in one of our rooms. We gave her the tour and she looked so exhausted, so I offered one of the rooms to her."

Well, isn't that fucking great?

"Are you ready for your tour?" she asks, her eyes lighting up at the prospect of showing off her place.

"Sure."

"Follow me," she instructs. "We're about to have our busy season. Fall in Carson is just breathtaking. We only have two other couples staying here right now. I can't show you their rooms, but if you'd like pictures we have them available on our website," she points out as we walk through a common area with a bar set up. She explains that they have beer and wine tastings on the weekends from some of the locals.

Through a French door, she takes me to the backyard which has a large covered patio and sprawling acres of grass set up with games, a pool, and a hot tub. Back inside, we cut through the modern kitchen before ending in the dining area. Then she takes me upstairs to the second floor where all but one of the guest rooms are located.

Around one of the corners is a hidden stairway that leads to the third floor, and what she calls her honeymoon suite. The bedroom spans the entire third floor with a full and open bathroom. A canopy floats above the bed, woven through the exposed beams of the ceiling. It's exactly what my brother and Elle would love.

"This is great. You've done a wonderful job restoring the home."

"Thank you very much," she replies warmly as we walk back down the third-floor stairs.

"Now I noticed that we've only toured the main section of the house. What are in the other two wings?"

"That is an excellent question. We also host a lot of events, so one wing is dedicated to that. The other is where my husband and I live. We like to be close enough to the guests, so if they need us we're not too far."

"I see." We stop in front of the door that Andrea indicated as the one where Sara is sleeping. "If you don't mind, I'm going to check on my friend."

"Sure, I'm going to start preparing the dinner. I do hope that you decide to stay for one night. Carson is a place unlike any you've ever been."

I smile at her retreating back and then turn to stare back at the door leading to Sara. With a soft hand I knock against the wood subtly and wait for a response, but when I get none, I slowly turn the knob on the door and open it a crack. Through the sliver, I whisper Sara's name, but all that returns is silence.

I pop my head through the small opening in the door and look around the sunlit room and find it empty and a bed fully made. But what really captures my attention is the hundreds of origami hearts scattered throughout the room like rose petals. I pick one up and inspect it closely noting how the heart isn't quite perfect, the folds are just a bit off center, but it so beautifully represents Sara.

A chair scratches from out on the balcony that I didn't notice when I first walked in and I see a figure relaxing with her dainty feet propped up on the railing. A drift of wind soars through the room bringing with it the clean smell of mountain air and a hint of the vanilla and honey fragrance I've grown to love.

She doesn't hear me approaching until I'm almost at the door, that's when she spins in her chair with a startled expression. Her hand rests on her chest as she works to catch her breath and I notice the five or six bandages adhered to her fingers and palms. Sara notices my gaze on her hand and she quickly tucks them behind her back as she stands.

"Hi," she whispers and I feel a sense of nervousness pulsing from her, as if she's afraid of my reaction to her.

"Hey," I respond and then I remember the small heart in my hand. "Uh, what are these?" I hold it up between my fingers as if she doesn't know what I'm referring to. She reaches out and takes it from me, that sweet blush that I love runs up her cheeks.

"Yeah, they're not quite perfect," she says with a forced chuckle. "I. . .ugh. . .wrote something on each of them," Sara tells me and I look back into the room in surprise. There are hundreds of them and now I'm eager to open each one, but at the same time opening each heart destroys the beauty on the outside.

Looking back at Sara still gripping the heart between her two fingers, I realize that perhaps she did this on purpose – to symbolize how her perfect exterior hides truths she keeps buried inside.

"What do they say?"

She shrugs and looks down at the heart in her hand, slowly pulling away one of the folds to reveal the crisp white interior. "Little nothings. Things I like about you, things that make me happy, apologies – like this one."

The slip of paper reads a simple handwritten note of "I'm sorry."

"What is all of this about, Sara?" I ask her, needing to know exactly what is running through her mind. She runs hot and cold so quickly that I never know which version I'm going to get. But something about her expression has me wanting to reach out and hold her close, this weary and afraid look in her eye is not one I've witnessed from her before.

Her tongue reaches out and licks those plump lips that I've been dreaming of every night since I first tasted them, and I want them more than ever right now. "I. . .um. . .wow this sounded so much better in my head."

"Just get it off your chest, Sara."

"I was hoping that I could convince you to stay the night with me. . .here."

I nod and pretend that I'm considering her proposal, but my heart and mind have already agreed and have her pinned to the bed and I'm making up for lost time. But I know that I can't do that. I have to make her realize how badly she has hurt me by stringing me along.

"Because you miss the sex?" I reply harshly and I internally cringe realizing how cruel that sounded even to my own ears.

Her hands which had been twisting the piece of paper within their grasp move to run through the golden locks of her hair and I physically ache to reach out and do the same.

"I miss you, Cooper. I miss being with you, laughing with you, even arguing with you. Until recently, I didn't know how much I hurt to keep people at a distance, there was a constant ache in my chest that never subsided. Never subsided until you.

"I don't know how to do any of this, I'm so focused on watching relationships crumble that I've never taken the time to see one blossom and grow. I want to try and I want you to be the one to teach me. Teach me that it's okay to argue and fight without the fear that it will lead to disaster. That one spat isn't going to have someone packing a bag and leaving.

"And I. . .I think you can teach me what love is. Or what it's supposed to be."

Sara bites down on her lip and looks at me with an eye of innocence I've never seen from her before. She's let that last wall down, that last barrier that kept her heart shielded and now it sits open and exposed. It's like I'm seeing her for the first time.

The silence draws out and her eyes dart away as the tension between us builds. But she doesn't look away fast enough to where I don't notice the lining of her lower lids fill with moisture. This crazy woman thinks I'm rejecting her.

Just as I'm about to squash her fears she whispers, "This was stupid. I'm just going to go and head back."

"Sara," I command as I call her name. She looks up at me with that same innocence, but also with a shadow of grief. And I hate that I've done this to her. I've put this melancholy inside this vivacious and independent woman. "Just stop talking."

As I shock her with my words, because no one tells Sara to stop talking, I place my hands on either side of her face and pull her mouth toward mine. Once our lips connect I vanish into this distinct feeling of being as one, of being home. She must feel the same because her hands grip my shirt, pulling me as close to her as our two bodies will allow, but it's still not enough. And though I wish that I could take her to the bed, or against the wall, or, fuck, right here in the middle of the room, I painstakingly pull away from her delicious mouth. With my hands still resting on her cheeks, I tilt my head down until our foreheads are touching

"I want this time to be different, Sara. This needs to be real this go round."

"That's what I want too. I'm done being afraid of having my heart broken."

"I'm not going to break your heart."

"How can you know that?" she murmurs.

"You just have to trust me."

"Okay. I can do that."

"Good. Now, what do you think about going downtown and exploring a little bit? Maybe we can get a recommendation from Andrea for dinner."

"Sounds like a great idea."

Removing my hands from her face, I lay them over hers still resting on my chest. Beneath my fingers, I feel the bandages, and it pains me to know that she caused so much damage to her fingers. Lifting each one to my lips, I press a gentle kiss on the tips, loving how her body shivers at the lightest of touches from me.

I shake my head as she moans my name and reminds her that we're going to explore and if I didn't know any better, I wouldn't be surprised if she stomps her foot like a sullen child being reprimanded.

Together we leave the room and wave to Andrea who is chatting on the porch with who I assume are some other guests. Even though she seems disappointed that we aren't staying for her meal, she recommends a local diner for our dinner. She winks in my direction and I suppose she has known all along that I would be staying the night.

The drive to the small downtown is quick and I park in an open parking lot on the far end.

"Carson really is cute. If I didn't love our town so much I could definitely see the appeal of moving here," Sara points out as she steps out of my car. I take a moment to admire her long legs only covered by a tiny pair of shorts.

"Maybe they need a lawyer in town." My suggestion seems to change something in Sara as she shrugs her shoulders and gazes down at the ground. I reach out and grasp her hand, trying my hardest to bring a smile back to her face. "Come on, maybe we can find something crazy to take back to Jackson and Elle. Oh, the weirdest thing happened while I was driving through here earlier." She gazes up at me as we walk waiting for my answer. "I am pretty sure that I saw the lead singer of Exoneration. I mean, it's crazy to think, but I had to do a double take."

She remains silent as we walk and I begin to think that I've something to upset her and just when I'm about to ask she pulls her hand free from mine and turns to face me. "I'm going to quit my job."

"What?" I ask in confusion, but then it dawns on me that I mentioned her job as a lawyer.

"I'm not happy there and I didn't work as hard as I have just to be handed everyone else's grunt work. And now that the practice is pretty much out of commission it's my perfect chance. Do you think I'm crazy?"

"Absolutely not."

As if she didn't hear my response, Sara continues to explain her decision by adding, "I mean, if I'm going to try and do relationships the right way I probably don't need to be surrounded by cynics, you know? And when we talked a few weeks back about me wanting to own a daycare, it really got me thinking that I should take the leap. I have money saved and I-," she continues, but I interrupt her with a soft kiss to her lips.

"I think it's a really smart decision, Sara. I support you one hundred percent."

"Really?" she says a bit breathlessly.

"Of course. And my offer still stands for you to move in with me while you go back to school."

"Well, I may take you up on that eventually, but I do have enough classes to safely take care of children in a facility, I would just need to go to school for the early education and business aspect. I already have a few places I'm looking into."

"If you moved in you wouldn't have to work and can focus on school. Just think about it. Now, I see a diner at the end of the road that is calling my name."

We walk hand in hand down the pathway taking our time to look in all of the storefront windows. A couple of older women standing in a fabric store eye me hungrily and I pick up my pace just a bit as we continue.

The diner comes into view and I hold the door for Sara to enter and also for a couple to exit as they wrangle their kids.

Inside the diner, I take a slow gaze around the classic décor and I admire how polished and new it looks.

We're greeted by a woman that seats us in a booth toward the back and suggests the meatloaf special since it's her specialty and we are new. The town must be pretty small if she can tell that we have never visited.

"So, tell me what you've been up to since I saw you last," Sara asks me as she takes a sip of her sweet tea.

"A lot of paperwork. Since the explosion at your work, we've been neck deep in charges and motives and bookings. But it's been exciting too. You know that our town doesn't have a lot of crime, so when we do have something happen it makes it interesting. I still wish that I could strangle that kid for hurting you though."

"I wasn't hurt that terribly."

"Sweetheart, I would have strangled him if you only broke a nail getting out of there. What he did was stupid and you could have been hurt so much worse." A shiver passes down my spine thinking about all of those hours I spent at the hospital waiting to hear the extent of her injuries and how badly she was wounded. "I'm pretty sure that I lost a few years of my life the moment when Elle called me that day."

Sara must realize that my mind has gone back to that day because she reaches out one of her bandaged hands and rests it over mine. I quickly turn my hand over so that I can hold hers in my grasp.

"I think that moment made me realize what I was capable of losing, which is why I had the kneejerk reaction to pull away from you. I didn't want to cause you any more hurt than what you had experienced," she tells me, and I really want to shout how ridiculous she's being, but I don't. Instead, I squeeze her hand and stroke my thumb across her soft skin.

Our food arrives at the table and my eyebrows shoot up my forehead in surprise when I take in the size of the platter. There is enough food here to serve a family of four. I look at the waitress and ask her if this is the normal portion and she just smiles and walks away.

"I guess we'll have some leftovers to take back." Stabbing my fork in the gravy covered meat, I cut off a piece and bring it to my mouth. The simple flavors explode in my mouth and without even taking a breath I start to shove bite after bite into my mouth.

"This is really good," Sara says as she slowly takes another nibble, probably taking her time to enjoy the meal. I finally look up and take a short break from my shoveling motion. "You probably want to chew and not swallow it whole," she jokes as she points to my plate, which now has half of my meatloaf missing.

The waitress stops back by the table and asks us if we need anything, her attempt to hold back her chuckle as she eyes my plate isn't working.

"Just the recipe to this meatloaf," I tell her as I spear another bite.

"No can do, my friend. Just means you'll have to come back to visit."

Sara and I finished our meal long ago and we sit chatting about everything and nothing, our conversation flowing easily. Finally deciding that we've worn out our welcome, we leave the diner just as the sun begins to hang low in the sky.

As we walk along the other side of the street taking in the shops we can hear some music thumping each time the door to the bar opens. Our eyes lock and we silently agree to go inside and see what all of the fuss is about.

I'm not sure what I expected inside the smalltown bar, but when I step past the threshold, I'm definitely shocked to find a clean and modern setting instead of a grungy speakeasy.

"Wow," Sara says beside me, and I wonder if she visualized the same thing.

A jukebox sits along the wall, propped up next to a small stage and dance floor. Booths line the walls with a few freestanding tables in between. From my line of sight, I can see a couple of pool tables and dart boards through an adjoining room.

Sara reaches down and grabs my hand, pulling me toward a booth that opens up by the stage and instead of sitting opposite of me, she tucks herself right next to me. We're so close that our thighs and arms touch.

A young man stops by our table and takes our drink order; both of us opting for a local brew, and then leaves us to take in the growing crowd. Just as the man returns with our drinks a large group enters the bar. I notice the couple from earlier that I held the diner door for and trailing behind them is the man from earlier and a bigger man that looks a hell of a lot like the drummer from the same band.

"Sara, look over at the entrance. Tell me that isn't Ryker James and Harlan Jax from Exoneration."

She settles her stare on them as the group pulls a bunch of tables together in the center of the room.

"I don't know. Hmm . . .maybe."

"Look, you know that it's one of my favorite bands."

"Really?" she asks in surprise and I realize that it's not something we've ever discussed.

"Yes, and my favorite color is red."

"Mine is green and I'm a fan of them as well. Let's find out."

She slides from the booth before I can stop her and before I know it, she's pausing at the end of their table introducing herself and smiling at something one of the women says. Sara stands there for a minute or two before waving and coming back to the table, finding both of the beers gone because I needed to drink them to mask my embarrassment.

"You were right, it's them. See, most of the group is Ryker's brothers and sisters, including Cassidy who is a world-famous fashion designer. Harlan is married to her. Ryker is from here."

"Well, I'll be damned. And by the way, you're going to have to drive back to the B and B. I drank your beer to distract myself."

"That's fine," she says with a laugh as she flags down the server to order one beer, promising that it's her only one for the night.

One of the women from the large group skips over to the jukebox and presses buttons until her selection starts to play and she waves over her partner to dance.

George Strait's "I Cross My Heart" blares through the speakers and I can't help but push Sara out of the booth and tug her onto the dance floor. She curves into my arms as we sway to the beat of the song and I realize that this is the first time we've danced since that fateful night at the fraternity party years ago.

"I prefer this dance over last time," I tell her and I'm awarded her beaming smile as she agrees. "I still have a hard time comprehending that it was you all along," she reveals, her hand on my shoulder sliding across the back of my neck. "I heard about the big bust that happened and I could have been tangled up in that mess."

"Everything happens for a reason."

"I believe that more than ever, now."

We continue to rock to the beat of the music, even when the song changes to a faster tempo. I finally have Sara in my arms again and I'm not ready to let her go.

Chapter Fifteen

Sara

"I CAN'T BELIEVE I'M getting married today." I look up at Elle as she stares at herself in the full-length mirror. She looks like a vision in an ivory A-line dress draped in taffeta and lace. The bodice cuts in a sweetheart neckline and curves across her shoulders. Her hair hangs loosely in waves around her shoulders, Elle opting to go veil-less for the occasion.

Beside her, Kennedy sits on the floor with mountains of tulle from her princess-style dress surrounding her. In the mirror, Elle looks over to me and I can see the glisten of unshed tears in her eyes and I immediately rush over with a tissue in hand.

No tears today.

My own pale pink column gown swishes between my legs as I make my way over to her before the first tear falls. We spent almost an hour in the makeup chair and I will not allow her sentimental moment to ruin it.

"I can't believe you're going through it again," I try to joke but fail miserably.

"Sara," she condescends. "When you have the right person you'll change your tone."

As I gently blot away her tears I confess, "I think I already found him."

Elle grabs my wrist and halts my movements. "Cooper?"

"Yeah. When we went away for the weekend a couple of weeks ago, we had a major turning point. And I finally stopped worrying about the what ifs and I'm letting myself enjoy being with him."

"I'm so happy for you, Sara. I'm sorry I haven't been around much. I haven't been the best friend. But that's going to change soon. I've decided to take a contract with a small production bakery in town to produce my recipes. I'll still do my cakes and special desserts, but the big items I'll leave to them.

"I want to spend more time with Jackson and the kids, and we're hoping to add onto the family in the next few years. I don't want to miss out on that."

"I get it, Elle. I'm very happy for you. You know, Cooper is the one that put the bug in my head to quit my job. And once the idea was there, it festered until I finally couldn't stand it anymore and realized that I wasn't happy with my job anymore. Even though I wish more lawyers were advocates for kids involved in divorce, I know that I can't help everyone."

"I'm really happy for you, Sara." Elle reaches her arms around me, and we embrace, the feeling just as comforting as being with my family.

Pulling back she exclaims, "You know what? If you and Cooper stay together, we could end up as sisters."

"Whoa, slow down a bit. I'm not ready to discuss marriage yet. Let me take this leap of being in a full-fledged relationship first."

"Oh, shush, you're totally marriage material. You were married to your job, now you can just move that focus to your man."

As we wait for the ceremony to start I pop open a bottle of champagne and I pour us each a glass, offering a cup of apple juice to Kennedy as well. I confess to Elle that I'm worried that she won't like what we've done for the ceremony or reception, but she assures me that she'll love it. But regardless that little fear buries itself in my head.

After we finish our glass of sparkling wine a knock on the door sounds and a deep voice sounds on the other side – Cooper's voice.

"I have a little boy here that would like to see his mommy."

I open the door just a crack and peek my head out to find Cooper holding the hand of a tuxedo-clad Noah. And he looks so freaking adorable I can barely stand it.

"Don't you both look so handsome?" I tell Noah as I bend down and adjust the small boutonniere on his jacket. I don't make eye contact with Cooper because I know that I'll want to climb him like a jungle gym.

"I want to see my mommy," Noah tells me and I step back and allow him to enter before sliding out to the hall, closing the door behind me.

"Is he nervous?" I ask Cooper without making eye contact with him, but the stubborn man reaches out and grips my hip, tugging me closer to him.

"You are breathtaking, Sara. Absolutely stunning."

Heat fills my cheeks and I'm sure that my blush matches the color of my gown at his compliment, something I'm learning everyday to accept from him.

"You don't look too bad yourself. It's good to know that the Divers men can clean up so nicely."

He chuckles and tightens his hold on me. "What? Already planning another wedding? For us maybe?" he jokes.

How does this man sear me from the inside with just his words? His confidence in us is almost as much of a turn on as when he whispers the things he wants to do to my body.

"Cooper. . ."

Smartly changing the subject, he asks how Elle is doing and I do the same about Jackson, until a small figure steps out in the hall and takes his hand. Cooper kisses me gently on the cheek and heads back to the groomsmen dressing room just as Kerry steps into the hall.

"Ready?"

I few minutes later, I stand at the entrance to the ceremony room ready to walk down the aisle before Elle. Kerry nods her head at me indicating that it is my turn to walk. I turn my head and wish Elle good luck. She is walking down the aisle alone this time, things still rough with her parents. I am surprised they've actually shown up, they didn't RSVP, but I overheard Kerry in her headset say that they had arrived late.

Stepping down the aisle, I smile at a few of the guests that I recognize, trying to keep my attention away from the front of the room, but once I hit the halfway mark I fail miserably. I can feel his stare penetrating through every inch of my body and it draws my eyes up to him. We are locked, tethered, pulled. There is no escape from the magnetism between the two of us. I even feel that the wedding guests can sense the connection we have.

I make it to the front and take my place at the makeshift altar on the opposite side of the groomsmen.

Kennedy walks in next, tossing the flower petals in the air with such fanfare that the guests chuckle behind their hands. Luckily the preschooler takes her spot beside me after she hugs Jackson's leg and we wait in anticipation for Elle to make her entrance. I can imagine her standing there with adrenaline coursing through her veins, her hands shaking in excitement, and swaying back and forth on the tips of her toes.

Finally, she takes a step from behind the barrier and she looks more beautiful at this moment than I've ever seen her before. I don't waste any time turning my head to capture Jackson's reaction and I'm not disappointed. His breath catches in his throat and he stares at her in wonder before a grin larger than any I've ever witnessed grows on his face.

From the corner of my eye, I catch the gaze of his best man. Cooper is intently looking with the same marvel in his eye as Jackson, but it's not directed toward Elle, it's aimed toward me. The way he's looking at me causes something deep inside to shift, to change, to accept. I know without a doubt that I love him, that I don't want to ever be without him. He's the better part of my every day and I barely recognized it until this moment. He's given so much of himself to me and I've given very little to him in return, but now I can irrevocably give him something no one else has had a chance to capture – my heart.

A cough grabs my attention as Elle stands smiling at me with her arm stretched out for me to take her flowers.

Oops.

The rest of the ceremony flows flawlessly and before long Jackson and Elle are pronounced husband and wife as the crowd cheers on. Instead of allowing Elle to walk down the aisle, Jackson lifts her into his arms and carries her away as she laughs. The kids follow closely behind. Finally, Cooper and I come together front and center of the aisle and he kisses my other cheek before I slip my arm around his and we make our walk behind the couple.

Just as we pass the barrier, we turn the corner to find Elle and Jackson wrapped around each other while their kids have their backs turned in embarrassment. I begin to giggle but my arm is yanked by Cooper as he pulls me into a small alcove.

"I want to kiss you so bad right now," he claims as he rests one arm around my waist and the other skims up and down my bare back exposed by my dress.

"There is no one stopping you."

"I'm not sure I'll be able to stop."

"I'm okay with that. But we do have pictures in a little bit and about forty-five minutes until the cocktail hour is over."

He looks like he ponders it for a moment as his eyes scrape up and down my body before settling on my mouth. I can tell that he's trying to hold back, trying to keep himself from devouring me the way he would like.

"Ah, fuck it," he growls and his hand sweeps into my loose locks and tilts my head toward his.

His tongue instantly brushes against mine as he explores my mouth as if he's seeking a hidden treasure.

"Pictures, guys." We're interrupted by an uncomfortable looking Taylor as she keeps her head downward toward the tablet in her hand.

"We'll be there in a moment," Cooper tells her without taking his eyes away from mine. Hidden within their blue swirled depths is the look of endless promises. Promises not to intentionally break my heart. Promises to take care of me. Promises to love me. My heart kicks up its pace, the beats rapidly pulsing my blood through my veins heating my skin all over from the intensity of his gaze. A place I want to stay lost in. Unfortunately, Elle and Jackson step past us and give Cooper a knowing look before reminding us to have our photos taken.

Together we follow the commands of the photographer. Some of the pictures are just of Elle and Jackson, then of their new family, and some include me and Cooper. But after Elle and Jackson take the kids back to the bridal suite Cooper and I stay in the ceremonial room laughing at Noah's attempts at a joke during the photography session. It's not until we're about to head back to the suite to join my best friend that I realize the photographer has been snapping pictures of us alone.

"You make a lovely couple," he tells us and I blush from the compliment. "Perhaps you'll give me a call when you plan your wedding." He holds out a business card and I reach out to retrieve it realizing that the thought of being married to Cooper doesn't frighten me nearly as much as it did just hours ago. Actually, it doesn't frighten me at all. Instead I feel a sense of excitement at the prospect of being tied to him forever. I gaze over my shoulder to look back at him with a smile and he openly replies the same.

In the bridal suite we're served our own plates from the buffet and until that moment I hadn't realized how ravenous I truly am. I joke with Cooper and tell him that I bet he's wishing for that meatloaf platter we ate while in Carson and he goes on to tell Jackson how he and Elle have to stop at the diner and try the meal. They both seem excited to get away for a few nights before taking their family vacation. I also hope that they make good use of their time, because I need another kid to call me auntie.

Kerry pops her head into the suite and I wonder if she's had a chance to eat yet, but she quickly rushes to tell us that the DJ is ready to announce the party. She takes the hands of Noah and Kennedy and hands them over to Jackson's mom waiting just outside the door.

We stand just outside the entrance of the reception area waiting for our chance to enter when I ask Elle, "How does it feel?"

"It feels. . .magical," she says with a grin etched on her face that has stayed since she woke this morning.

"When you get a chance tell me what you think of the decorations."

Elle nods and Kerry indicates that it's time for me and Cooper to step into the hall. He holds my hand tightly, our fingers intertwined as if he's afraid I could slip away at any moment. But he has absolutely nothing to fear, I'm not going anywhere.

After we're all announced and the crowd cheers for Elle and Jackson we watch them move as one during their first dance. I take that moment to gaze at the decorations and I'm amazed. It looks exactly like something out of a magazine. In the corner, I spy the cake Cooper and I picked out and have to fight against my desire to burst out in laughter as I remember the fight we had at the cake shop.

"Thinking about the cake?" he whispers against my neck as he slips his arms around me from behind.

"Maybe." I don't tell him how I wish that I could go back to that day and lick the icing from his naked body, I keep that tidbit to myself.

"Must be a dirty thought." My back stiffens and I tilt my head back to look at him defiantly. But his thumb reaches out and traces a line across my forehead. "You have a vein here that pops out when you're thinking about something dirty. It's one of my favorite things about you."

Talk about being transparent with your emotions. I can't hide when I'm turned on or embarrassed.

"I want to dance with you," he murmurs as he reaches down for my hand, trailing his fingers down my arm until he reaches his intended destination.

"They're going to cut the cake soon."

"I know."

I see my brother sitting with Hunter at a table near the stage and he eyes Cooper's hand laced with mine and I'm afraid he's going to cause a scene. My brother may be younger and I spent a lot of my younger years protecting him, now he thinks he has to do the same for me. I find myself doing a double take when he nods at Cooper then takes a sip of his whiskey. I'm not sure what just happened but it seems as if my brother has given Cooper his seal of approval.

My curiosity demands that I ask Cooper about it, but once we reach the dance floor shared by a few other couples he twirls me into his arms and I laugh at the grandness of the motion and forget everything else on my mind slipping away.

We sway to the beat of the popular song and when it ends I expect Cooper to take a step back, but instead, he pulls me closer. Then, as if he requested it, the song by George Strait that we danced to at the bar in Carson begins to play. The emotions flood through me and I blink quickly to mask the tears flooding my eyes and I smile a watery grin at Cooper.

"Cooper. . ." I whisper, unable to put into words the way that I'm feeling at the moment, the way that I feel about him at this moment. Until a light bulb goes off in my mind and I know exactly what to say, a truth I've been hiding from him for days. "I love you."

His sexy grin turns into a full wattage smile. "I love you, Sara." Cooper dips his head and kisses me in front of our friends and his family with a passion unleashed for the first time. We continue that way through the remainder of the song, barely pulling apart enough to take a breath, and as we take a small step away I'm awarded that sexy grin I love so much.

"What?" I ask the man that looks like he's harboring some devilish secret.

"I told you that you were mine."

Epilogue

Sara

"THIS IS THE LAST one," Hunter grunts as he plops the last of my moving boxes on the floor of the living room. When I started packing up my condo, I was surprised at how many items I had accumulated throughout the years. Knickknacks, toys, magazines, I kept a little of everything, not quite hoarder level, but I wasn't too far away. Luckily, the move to Cooper's house was a nice time to purge everything.

About a day after the wedding Cooper didn't waste much time in convincing me to move in with him. All he had to do was withhold an orgasm and I was ready to commit. He was disappointed when it didn't happen right away – eight months to be exact. I wanted to get my condo situated and that meant renting it out, currently to the man that is sifting through my boxes, but he was tied into his lease.

"Hunter, what are you doing?" I ask as he flips the folds of one of the boxes open.

The stubborn man reaches into the box and pulls out a stack of paper and stares at it incredulously. "You packed paper?"

I snatch the stack from his fingers and place it back into the box. "It's origami paper. Why don't you go back to your new place?"

"Ah, come on. You know that you love my company." Normally, yes I do, but today I just want to be alone with Cooper before we meet with Jackson and Elle for dinner.

His cell phone pulls his attention from me as he tugs it from his pocket and looks down at the screen.

"Actually, I have to go. I'll meet you there tonight."

"Remind me again why you're coming to talk about a baby shower."

Hunter looks up at me like I've grown two heads. "Woman, I will not let that baby boy have a girlie baby shower. I need to be there to make sure we stay on track."

"Don't be so barbaric, Hunter."

The stubborn man grunts as he leaves the house and I go back to organizing the boxes and carrying them to the room they belong in. I've already moved my clothes into the closet and dresser, and Cooper has given me free rein to update the bedroom, but I actually like it the way it is. All I add is a soft white blanket on the edge of the bed. The rest of my furniture I left for Hunter.

Cooper had to go into the office this morning to finish up one of the cases he had been working on, which is why Hunter was nominated against his will to help me.

In the kitchen, I start pulling out my pots and utensils, placing them alongside Cooper's and I feel a sense of warmth spread through me having my things mixed with his. After a few hours, I've tackled the kitchen and most of the living room. Placing a picture of Elle and me on the built-in bookshelves I look over at a picture of Cooper and me from the wedding.

In the image, I'm looking over at something with a smile on my face, my small bouquet of flowers dangling at my side while my other hand is tightly encased by Cooper's. But it's Cooper's expression that wrecks me every time that I look at the picture. He's looking at me as if I'm an angel sent from heaven just for him; a gift, a treasure, a prize. There is so much love pouring from him in a single look that shivers trickle down my spine every time I look at it.

I run my finger across the glass tracing his face with my touch. That day was one of the best of my life.

"I love that picture." Cooper startles me as he sneaks into the house. I take a moment to catch my breath before turning around. He stands there looking sexier than ever in his leather jacket, dark jeans, and smoldering grin. One of his arms is tucked behind his back and my curiosity rises.

"Hey, how was work?" I greet him and press my lips against his, savoring the warmth of his kiss.

"Boring. Are you all moved in?"

"For the most part. What are you hiding?"

Cooper shrugs and then grabs my hand, drawing me toward the bedroom.

"I have these for you." He holds out a bouquet of flowers, and not just any flowers, beautiful origami flowers shaped like roses.

"These are gorgeous, Cooper." A glimmer in one of the roses catches my eye and I peer inside the center of each rose and notice a different colored gemstone glued to the centers. All different colors are scattered throughout, but the flower on the top has me taking a second glance as I look inside.

A ring.

And not just any ring, a diamond ring with a large center stone with smaller stones in alternating sizes wrapped around. It looks like a flower and it's one of the most stunning rings I have ever seen.

Cooper takes the flowers from me and reaches inside the paper bloom to retrieve the ring. And I should have expected it, and maybe I did, but I'm still in shock.

He kneels before me and with a shaking hand, he reaches out to hold one of mine while lifting the ring in the air between us.

My pulse is echoing through my ears that I'm not even sure what Cooper is saying besides that he loves me and that he can't see himself growing older with anyone else.

I never imagined that I would allow myself to open up with someone the way that I have with him, or would find myself falling more in love with a man every single day. This man that I used to dream about strangling is the same man that I now dream about creating a family with.

So deep in my heart, I know that there is no one else I would rather take this leap of faith with. No one else I want to travel along this new journey.

"Sara, will you marry me?"

I can tell that he's nervous, our rocky start and my fears still sitting on the back burner in his mind. I don't purposefully pause dramatically, but when I try to reply my mouth is drier than the Sahara Desert.

I force myself to lick my lips and try again.

"Yes. Without a doubt, I want to be your wife."

He pulls us together as he stands up and slips the ring on my finger.

"Really? You're going to marry me?"

"I really am." I grin at him.

"Fuck yes!" he quips in joy before slamming his mouth against mine and then pulling away. "Now, take your clothes off."

"What?" I ask as he completely switches gears.

"Yes, I want to make love to my fiancée wearing nothing but my ring."

"Oh, well if you insist."

Acknowledgements

Enormous thanks to my team. Renee, Virginia, Wander, Lisa, Amanda, Crystal, and Sally, Heather, Teri, Kristine, and Thia, Sierra, Samantha, and Jen – you guys are absolutely amazing and I am honored that I get to work with you.

To my readers I send so much love and thanks your way. I appreciate the love and support you give me and my books.

Thank you to my family for always supporting me and allowing me to follow my dreams.

About the Author

Renee Harless is a romance writer with an affinity for wine and a passion for telling a good story.

Renee Harless, her husband, and children live in Blue Ridge Mountains of Virginia. She studied Communication, specifically Public Relations, at Radford University.

Growing up, Renee always found a way to pursue her creativity. It began by watching endless runs of White Christmas- yes even in the summer – and learning every word and dance from the movie. She could still sing "Sister Sister" if requested. In high school, she joined the show choir and a community theatre group, The Troubadours. After marrying the man of her dreams and moving from her hometown she sought out a different artistic outlet – writing.

To say that Renee is a romance addict would be an understatement. When she isn't chasing her toddler or preschooler around the house, working her day job, or writing, she jumps head first into a romance novel.

Reader group: Renee Harless' Risque Readers
https://www.facebook.com/groups/reneeharlessrisquereaders/
Facebook: facebook.com/authorreneeharless
Amazon: www.amazon.com/Renee-Harless/e/B00VAHGAWE
Bookbub: www.bookbub.com/authors/renee-harless
Newsletter: www.reneeharless.com/newsletter
Instagram: @Renee_harless
Tiktok: @authorreneeharless